MINIONS

EVIL PANIC!

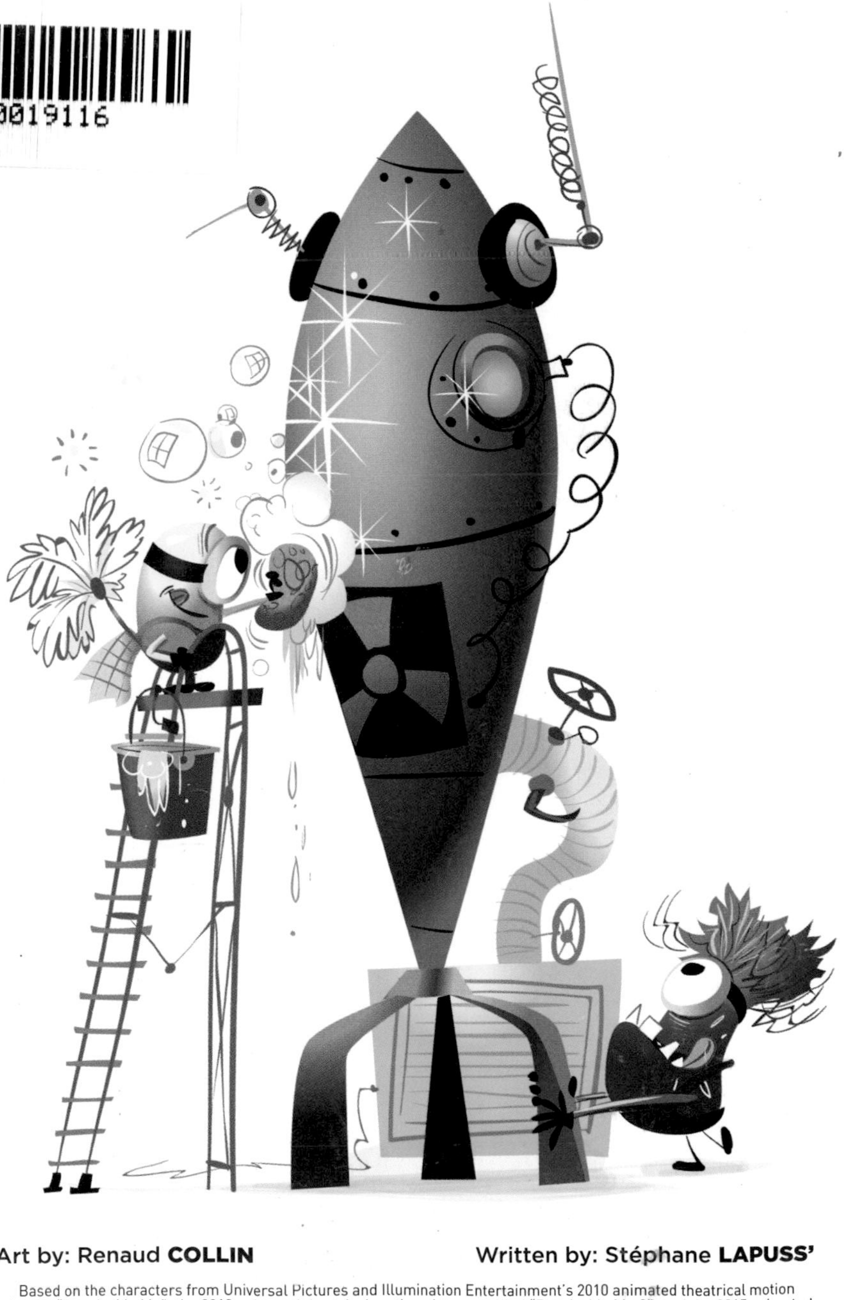

Art by: Renaud **COLLIN**

Written by: Stéphane **LAPUSS'**

Based on the characters from Universal Pictures and Illumination Entertainment's 2010 animated theatrical motion picture, "Despicable Me", the 2013 animated theatrical motion picture entitled "Despicable Me 2", and the 2015 animated theatrical motion picture release presently entitled "Minions".

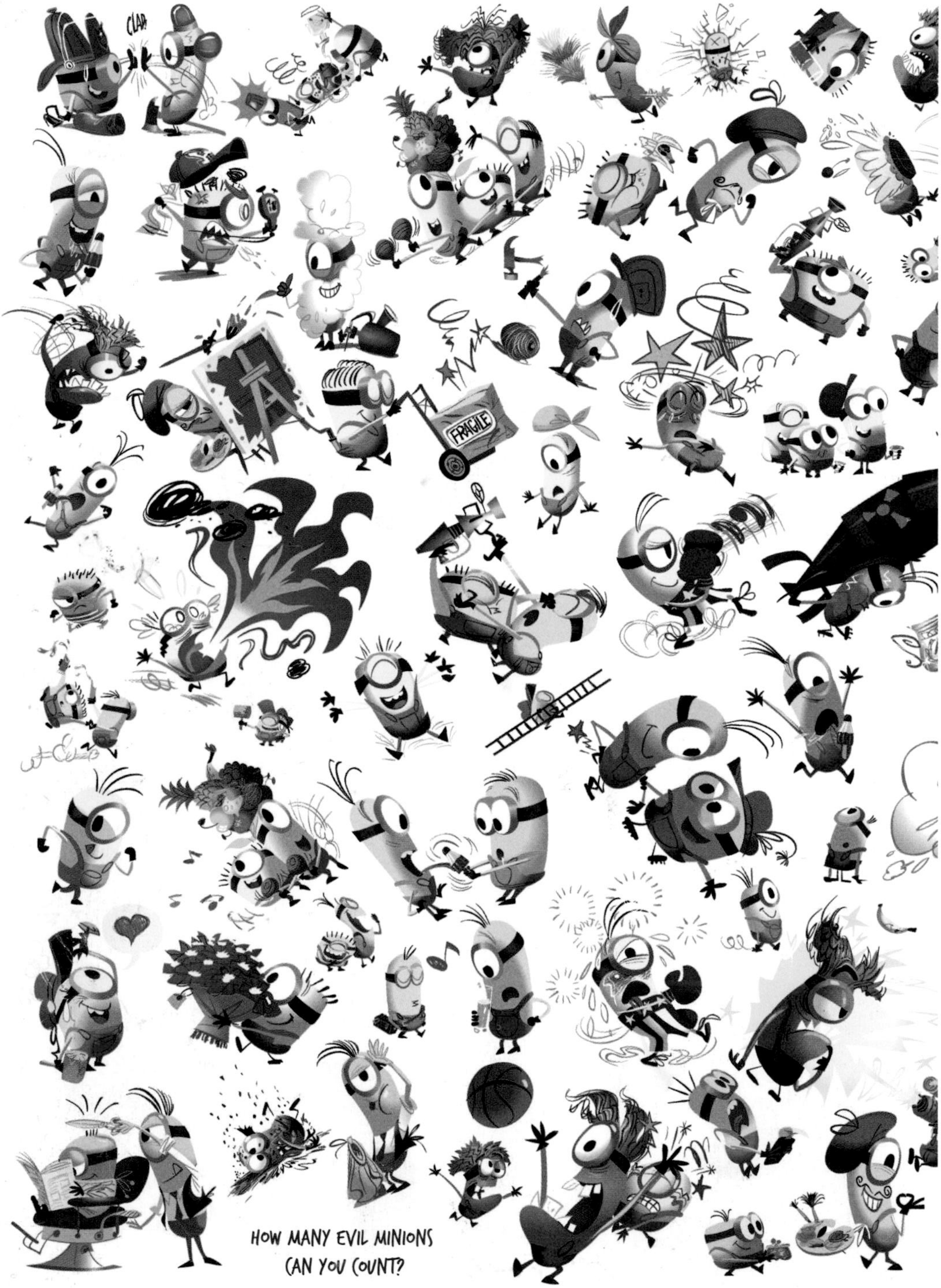
CLAP!
FRAGILE

HOW MANY EVIL MINIONS
CAN YOU COUNT?

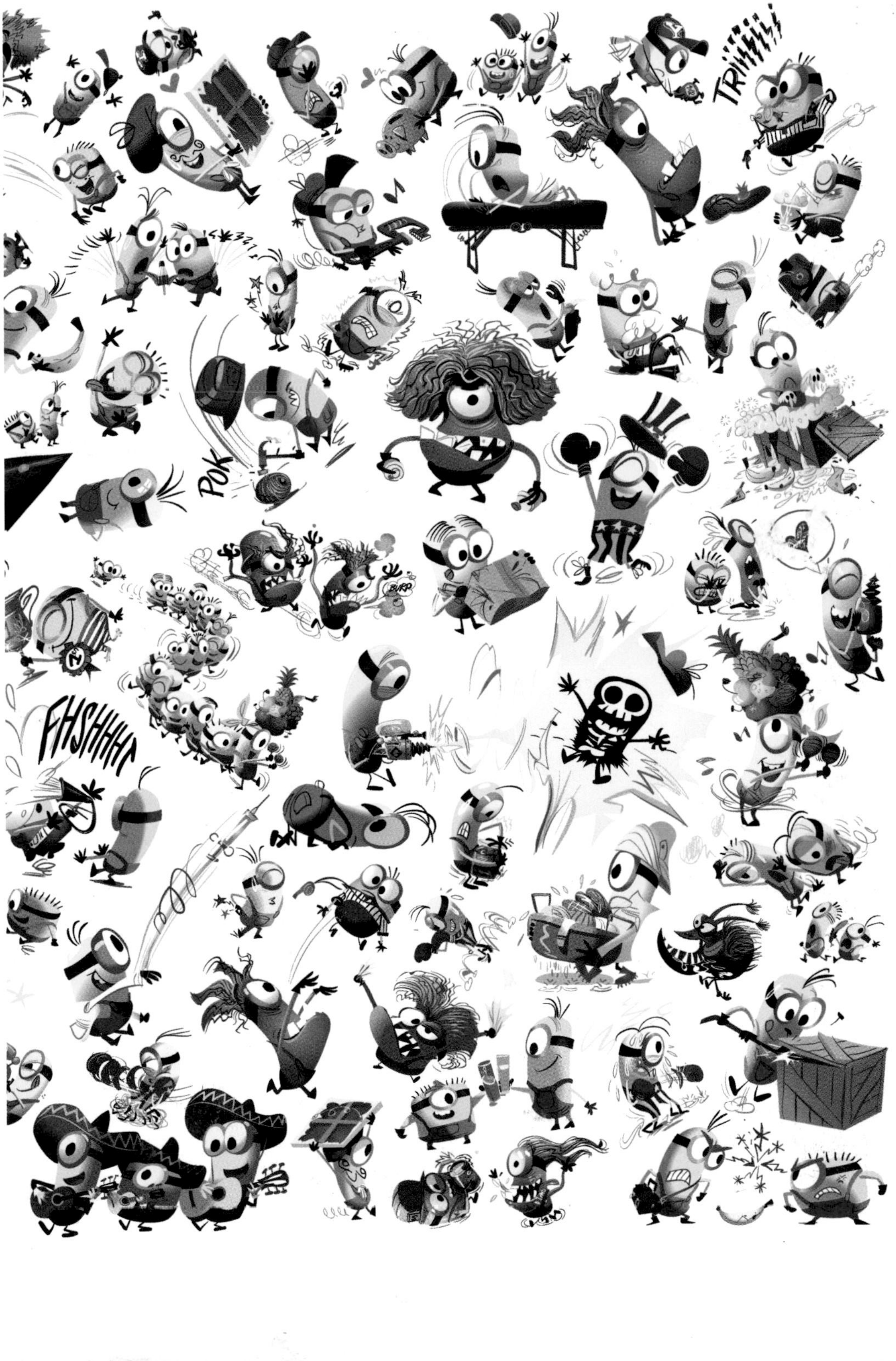
POK
BURP
FHSHHHT

TITAN COMICS

Senior Editor
NATALIE CLUBB

Senior Designer
EMILY NORRIS

Studio Manager
SELINA JUNEJA

Production Supervisors
PETER JAMES, JACKIE FLOOK
MARIA PEARSON

Production Manager
OBI ONUORA

Senior Sales Manager
STEVE TOTHILL

Commercial Manager
MICHELLE FAIRLAMB

Direct Sales & Marketing Manager
RICKY CLAYDON

Publishing Manager
DARRYL TOTHILL

Publishing Director
CHRIS TEATHER

Operations Director
LEIGH BAULCH

Executive Director
VIVIAN CHEUNG

Publisher
NICK LANDAU

Bookstore ISBN: 9781782765554
Scholastic ISBN: 9781785851827

Published by Titan Comics,
a division of Titan Publishing Group Ltd.
144 Southwark St. London, SE1 0UP

Based on the characters from Universal Pictures and Illumination Entertainment's 2010 animated theatrical motion picture, "Despicable Me", the 2013 animated theatrical motion picture entitled "Despicable Me 2", and the 2015 animated theatrical motion picture release presently entitled "Minions".

10 9 8 7 6 5 4 3 2 1
Printed in USA by RRD, November 2015
A CIP catalogue record for this title is available from the British Library.
Titan Comics. TCN0859

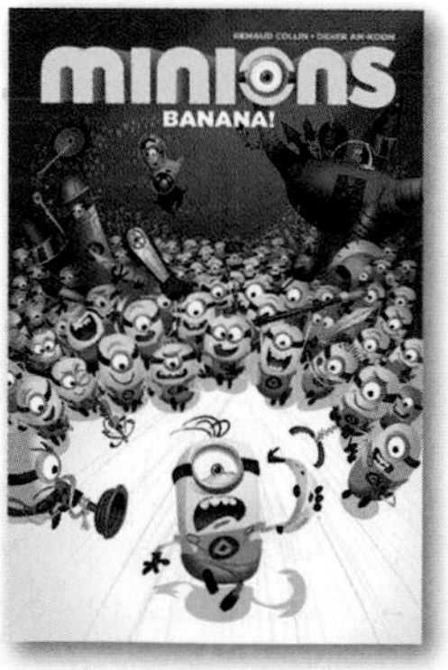

MINIONS
BANANA!

EVIL MINION

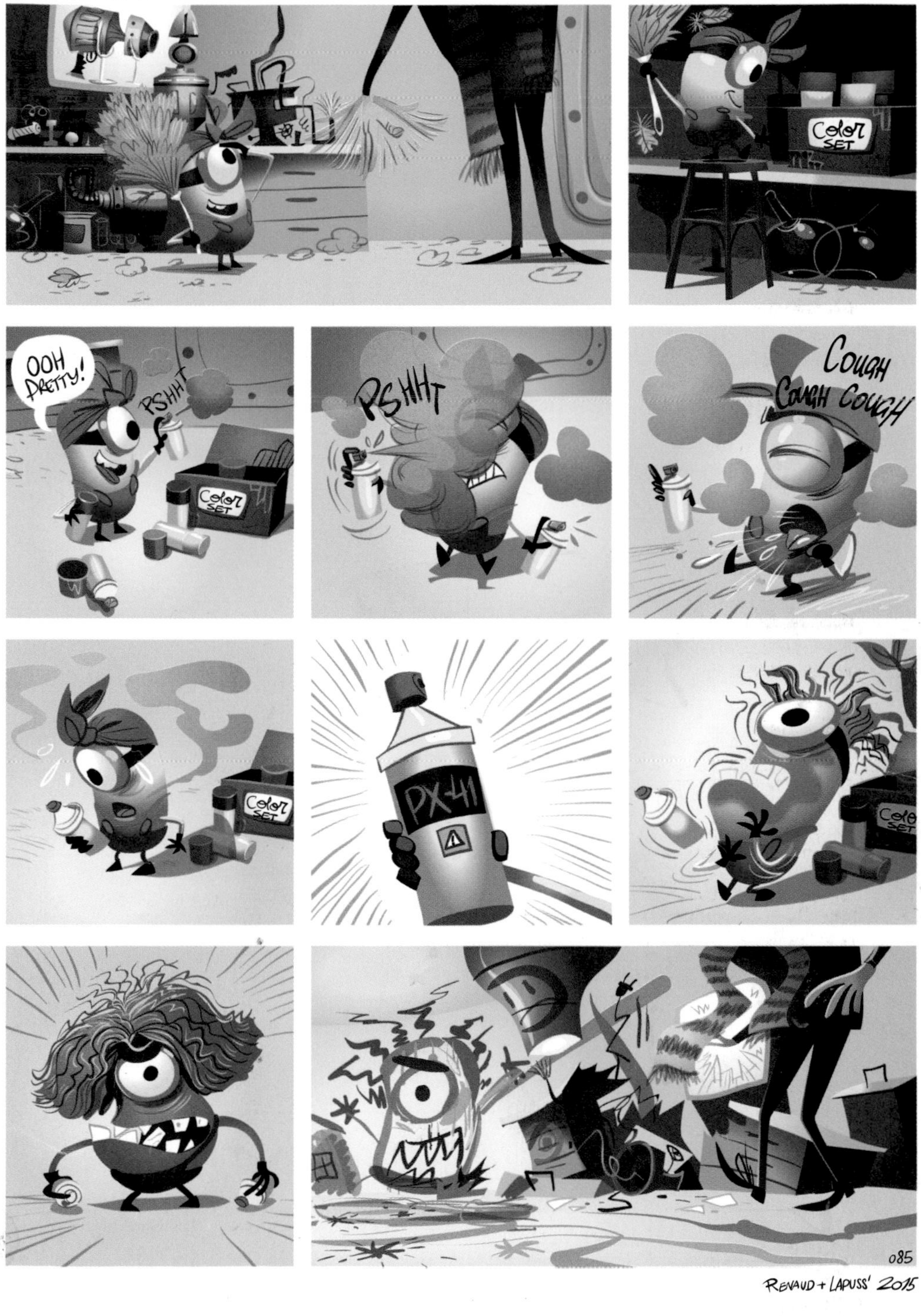
Color SET
OOH PRETTY!
PSHHT
Color SET
PSHHT
COUGH
COUGH COUGH
Color SET
PX-41
Color SET

RENAUD + LAPUSS' 2015

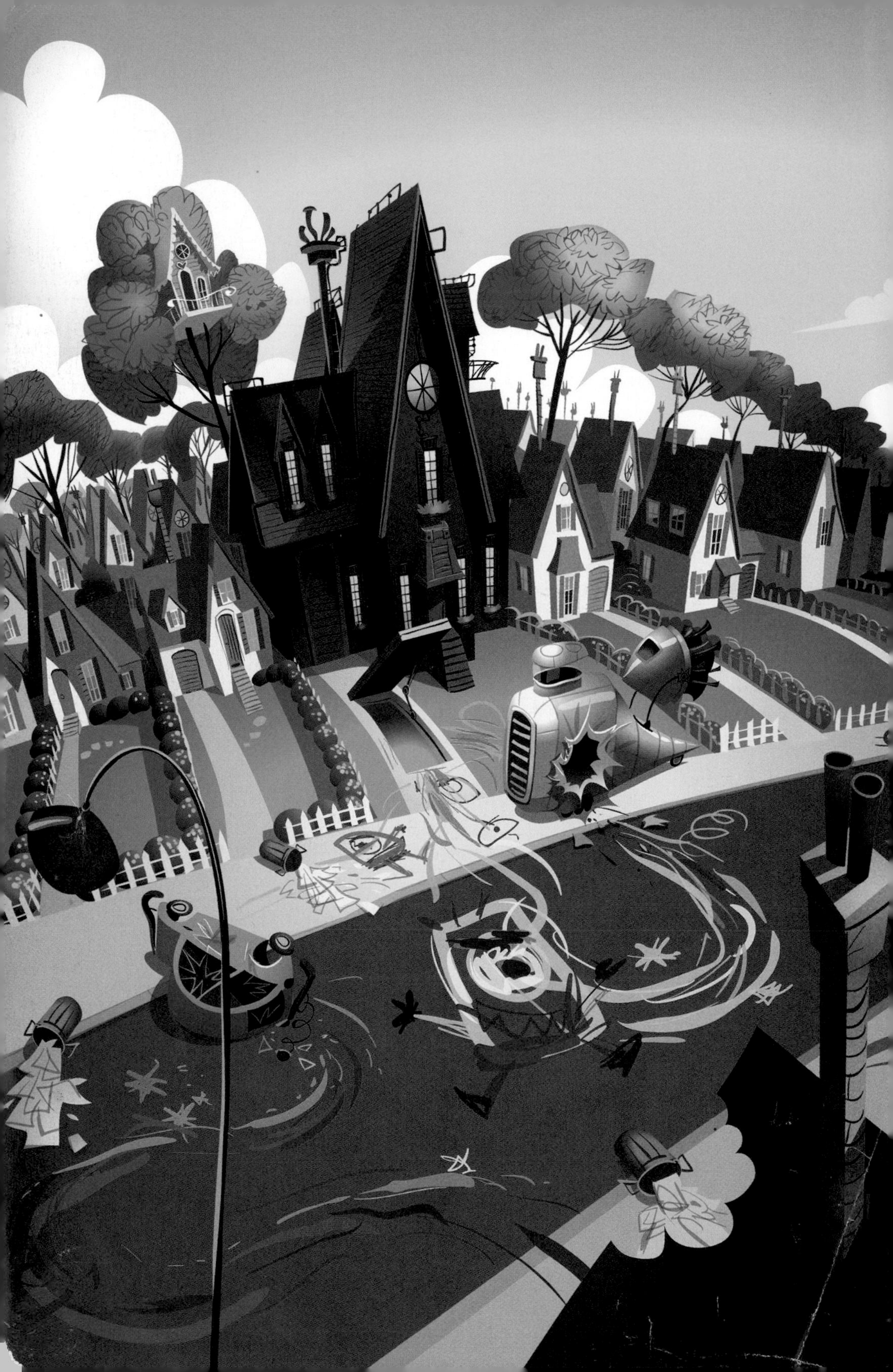

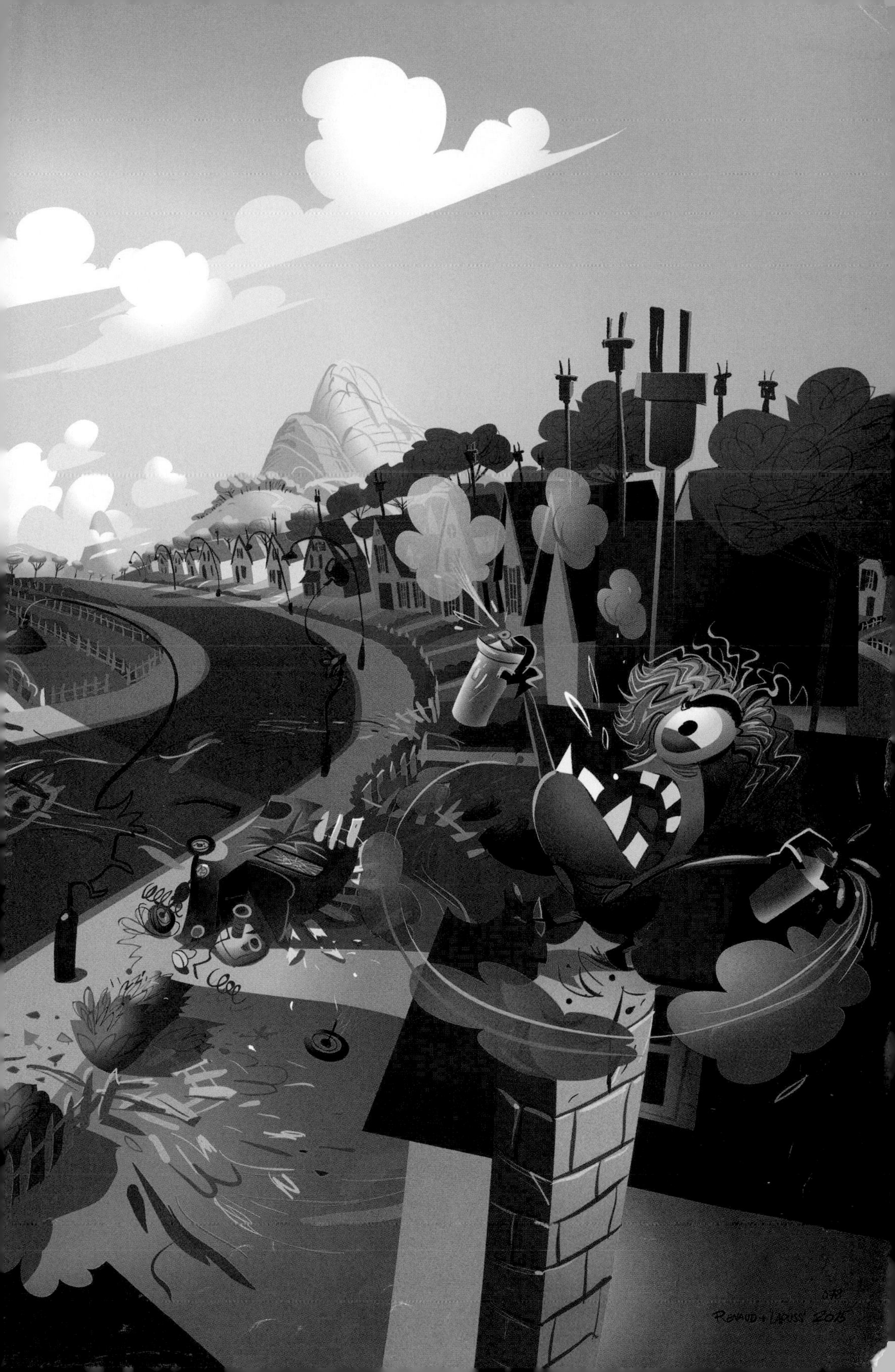

AN EYE FOR AN EYE

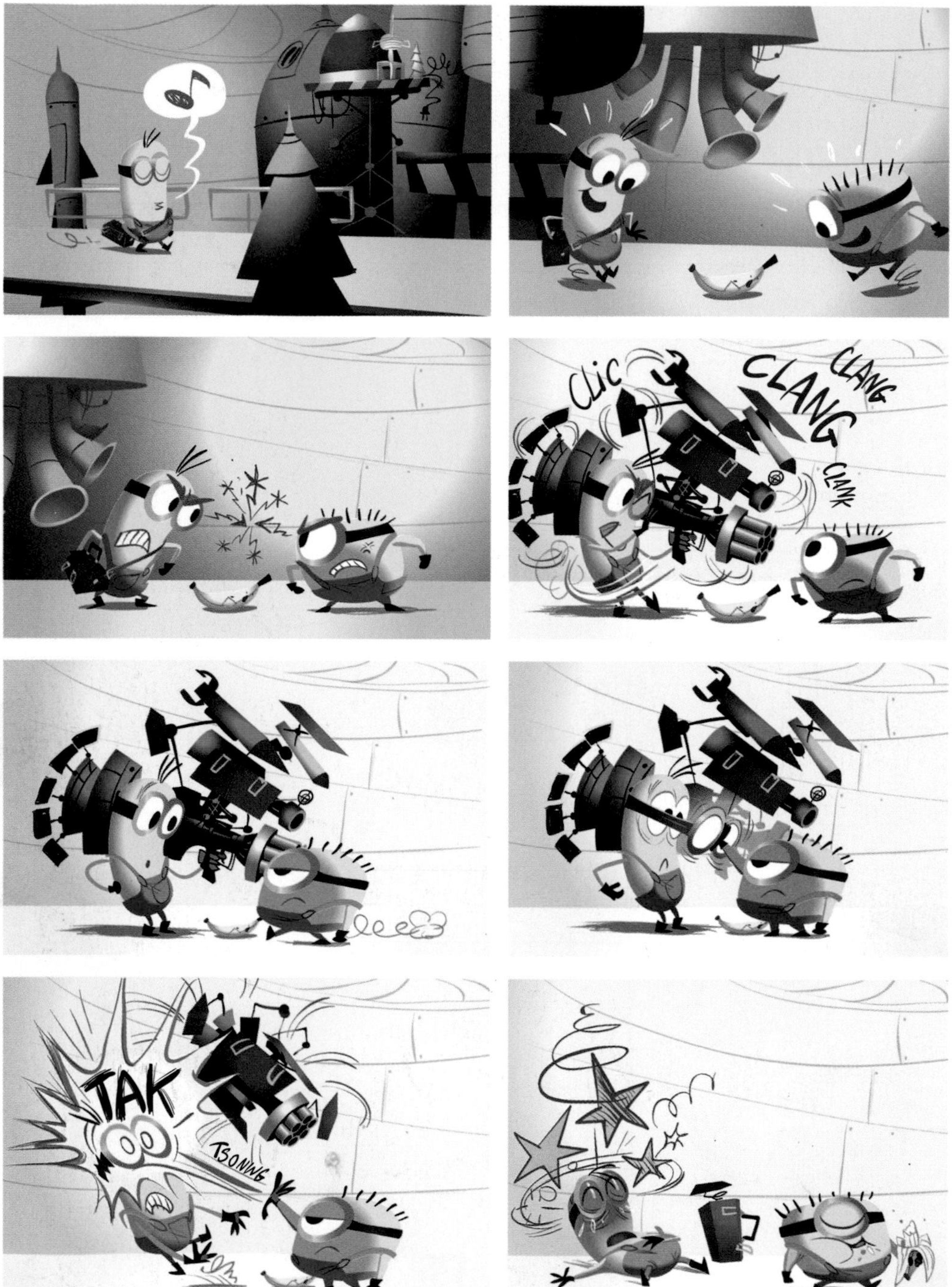
CLIC
CLANG
CLANG
CLANK
TAK
TSOINNG

RENAUD + LAPUSS' 2015

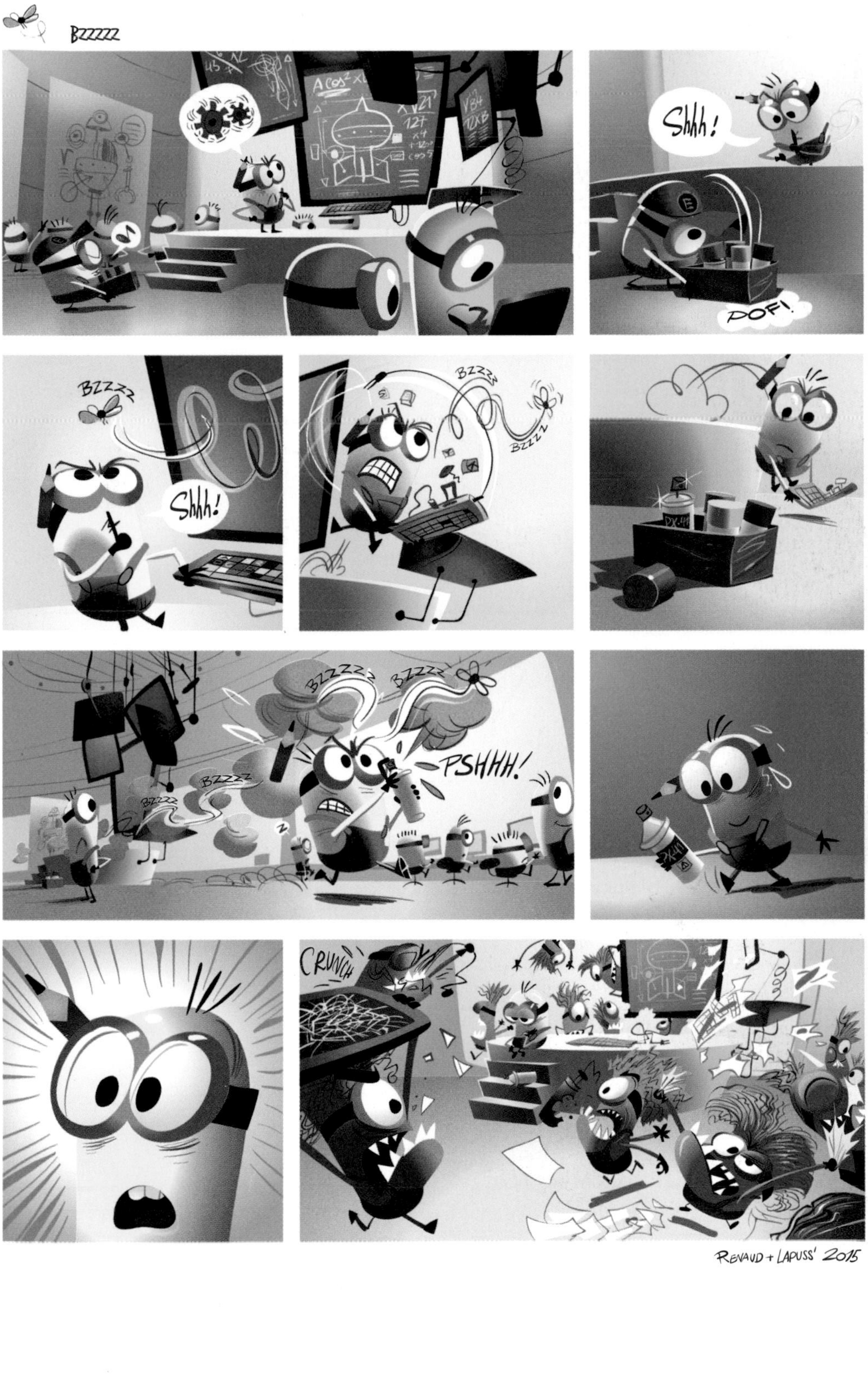
BZZZZZ
Shhh!
POF!
BZZZZ
Shhh!
BZZZZ
BZZZZ
BZZZZZ
BZZZZ
PSHHH!
BZZZZ
BZZZZ
CRUNCH
RENAUD + LAPUSS' 2015

CHEERS!

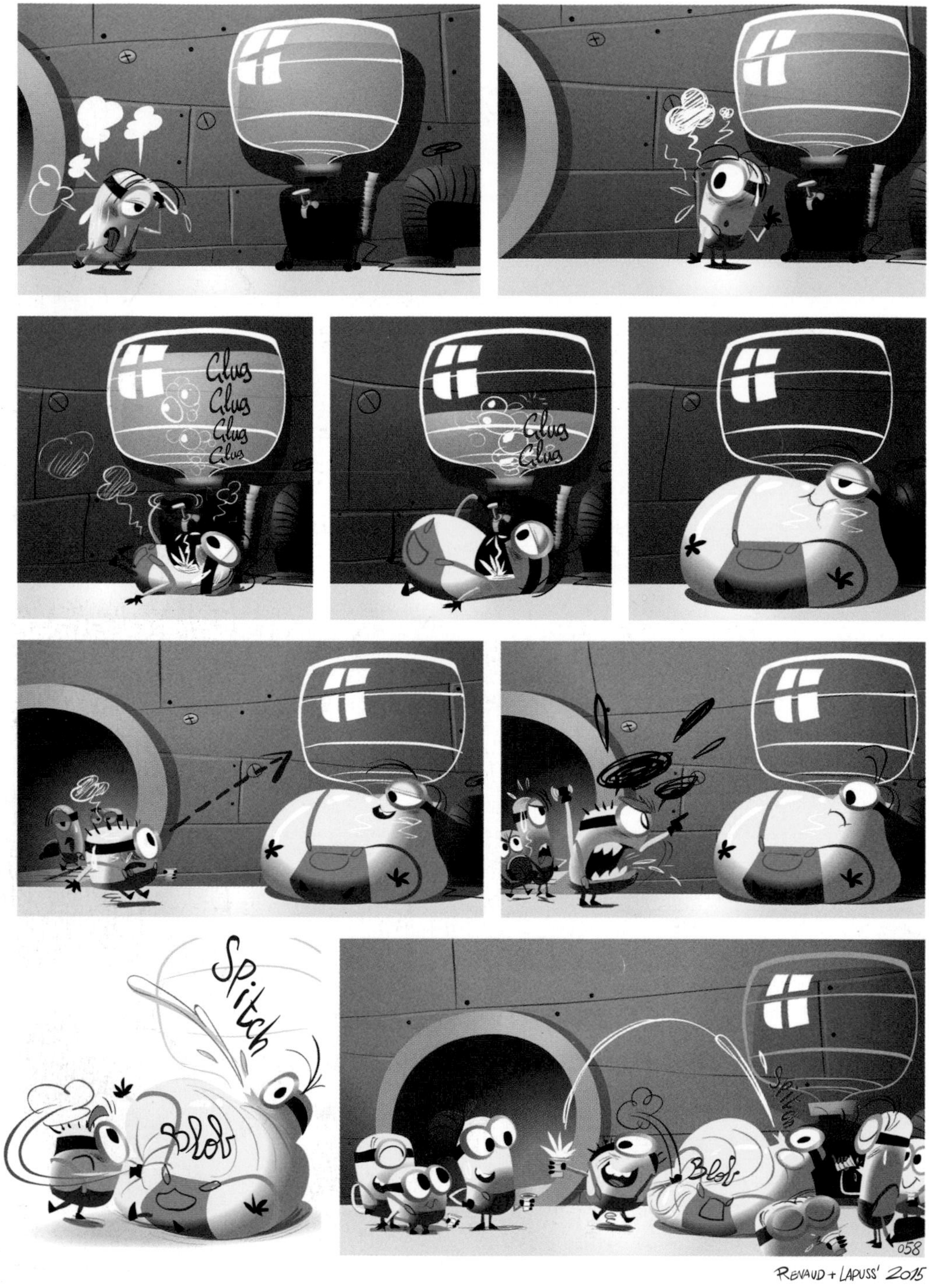

Glug
Glug
Glug
Glug
Glug
Glug
Spitch
Blob
Blob
058

RENAUD + LAPUSS' 2015

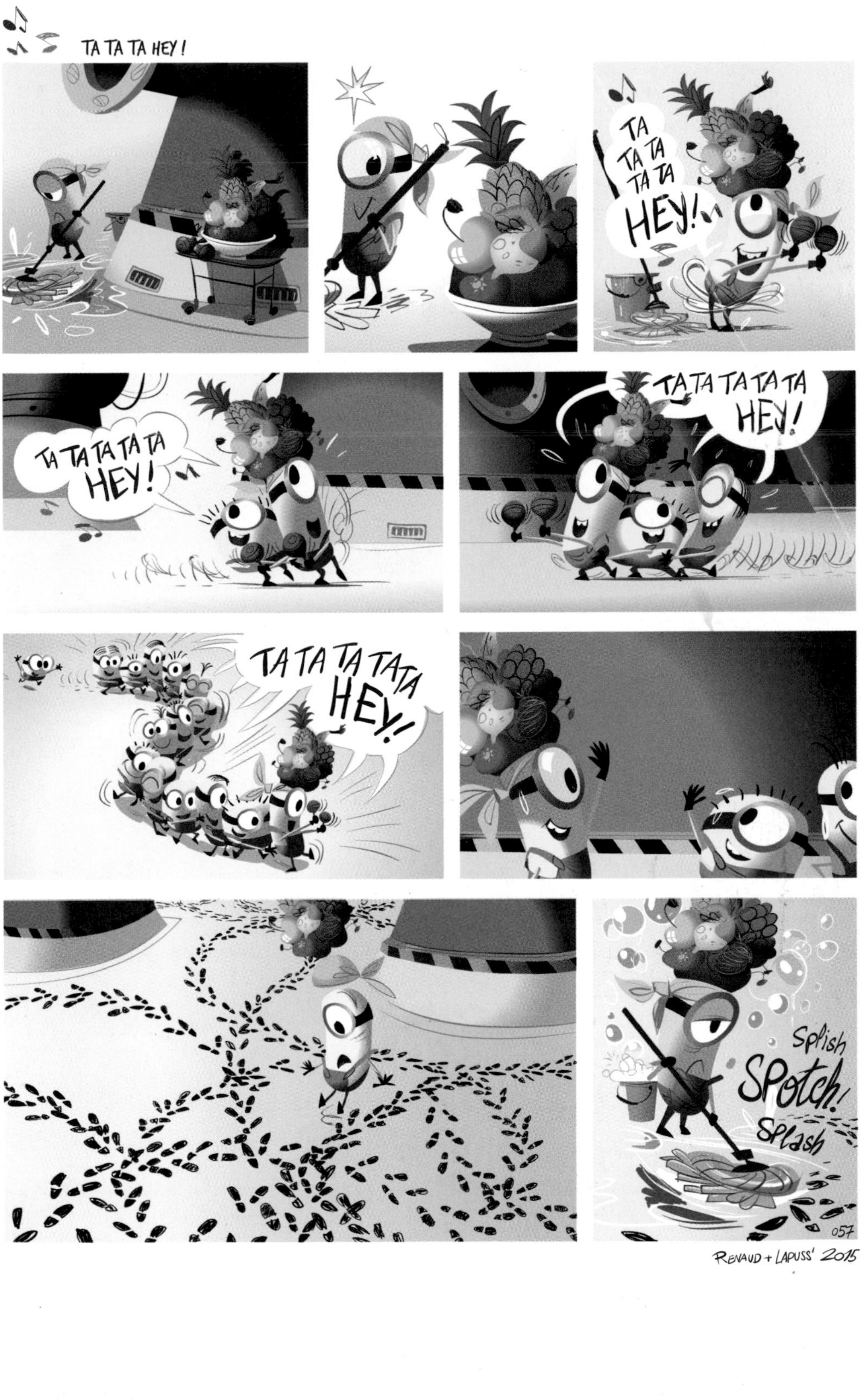
TA TA TA HEY!
TA TA TA TA TA HEY!
TA TA TA TA TA HEY!
TA TA TA TA TA TA HEY!
TA TA TA TA TATA HEY!
Splish
SPotch!
Splash
057
RENAUD + LAPUSS' 2015

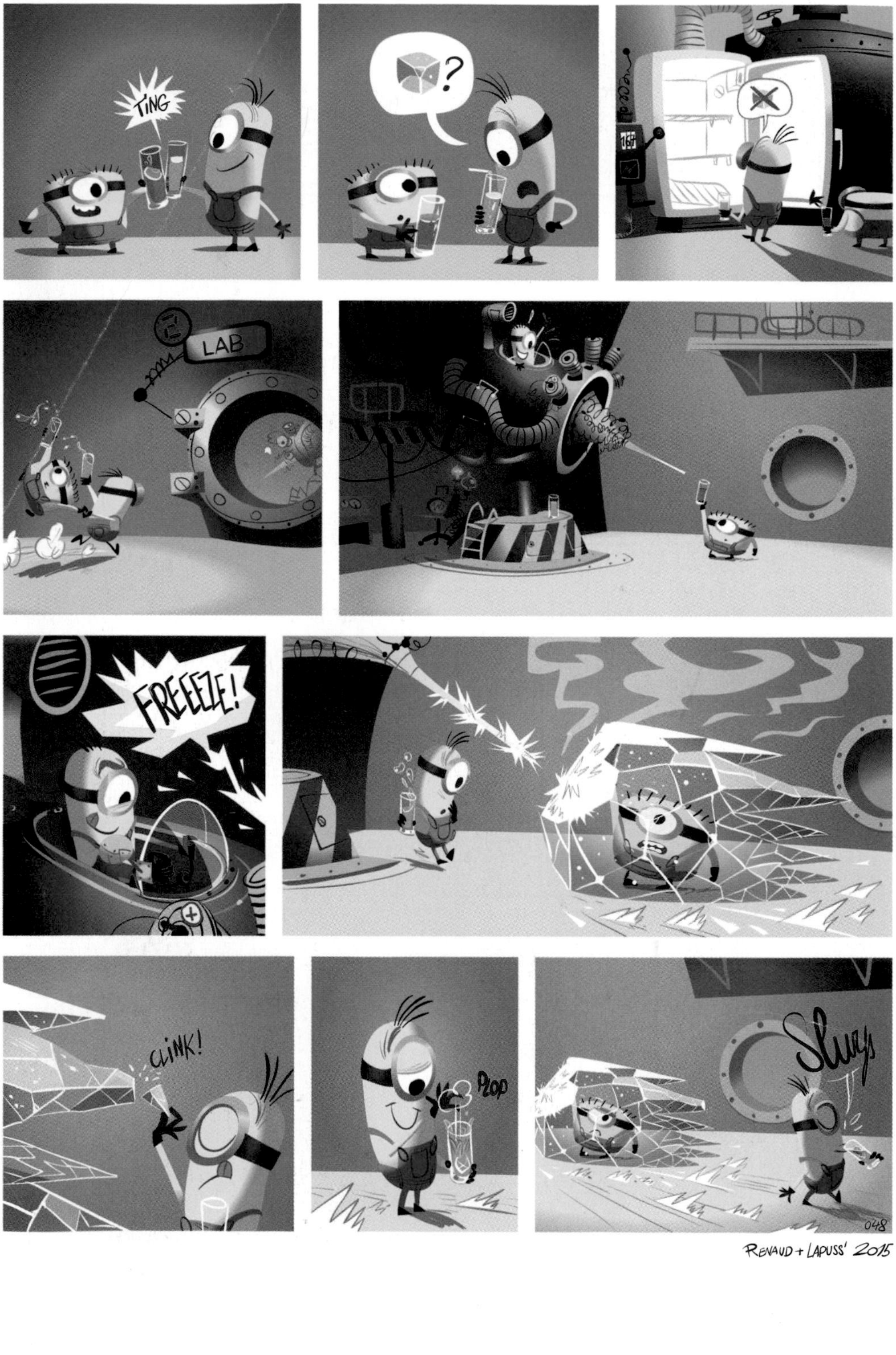
TING
?
LAB
FREEEZE!
CLINK!
PLOP

RENAUD + LAPUSS' 2015

BBQ PARTY

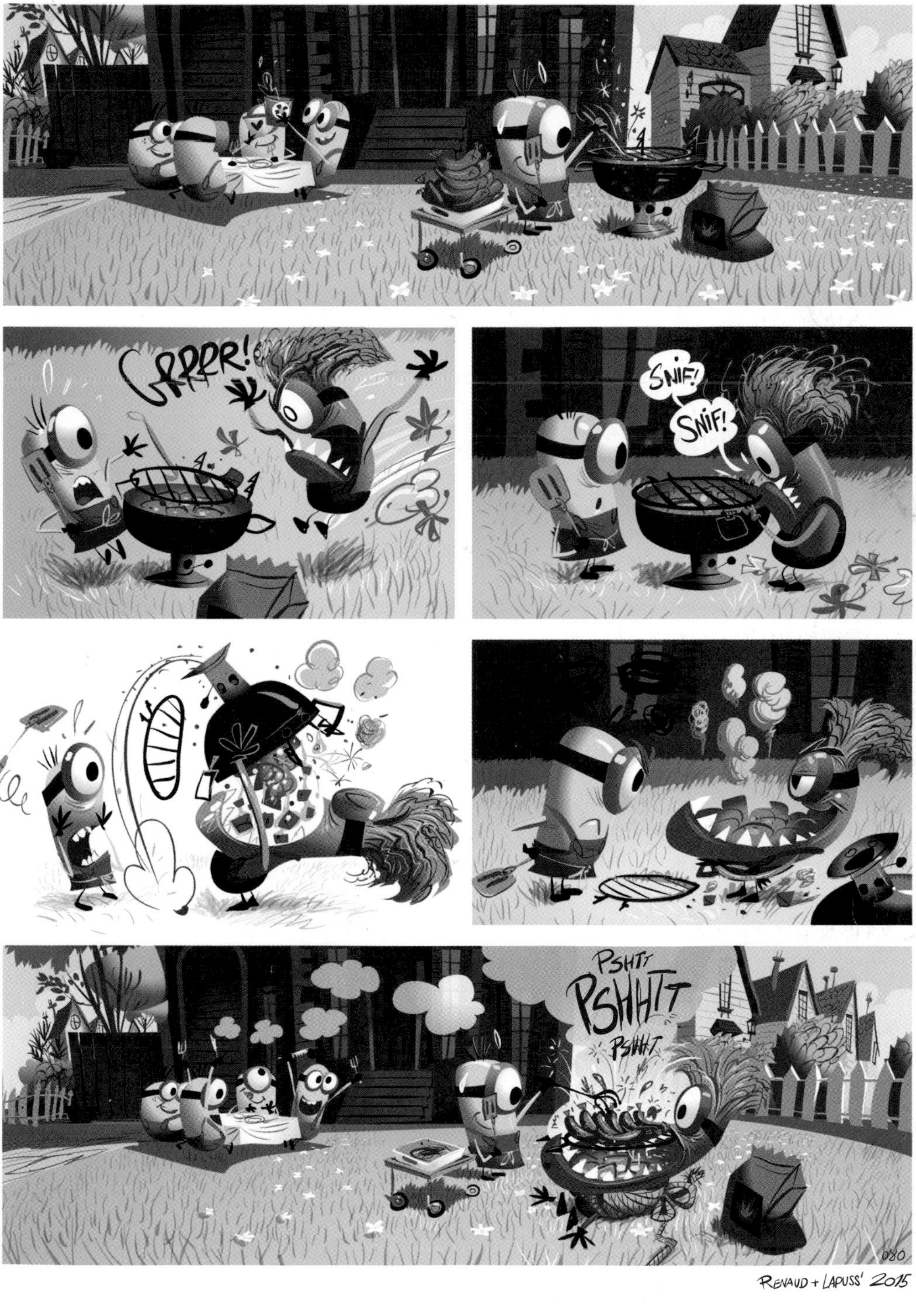

GRRRR!
SNIF!
SNIF!
PSHTT
PSHHTT
PSHHT
080

RENAUD + LAPUSS' 2015

FRAGILE HOPELA !

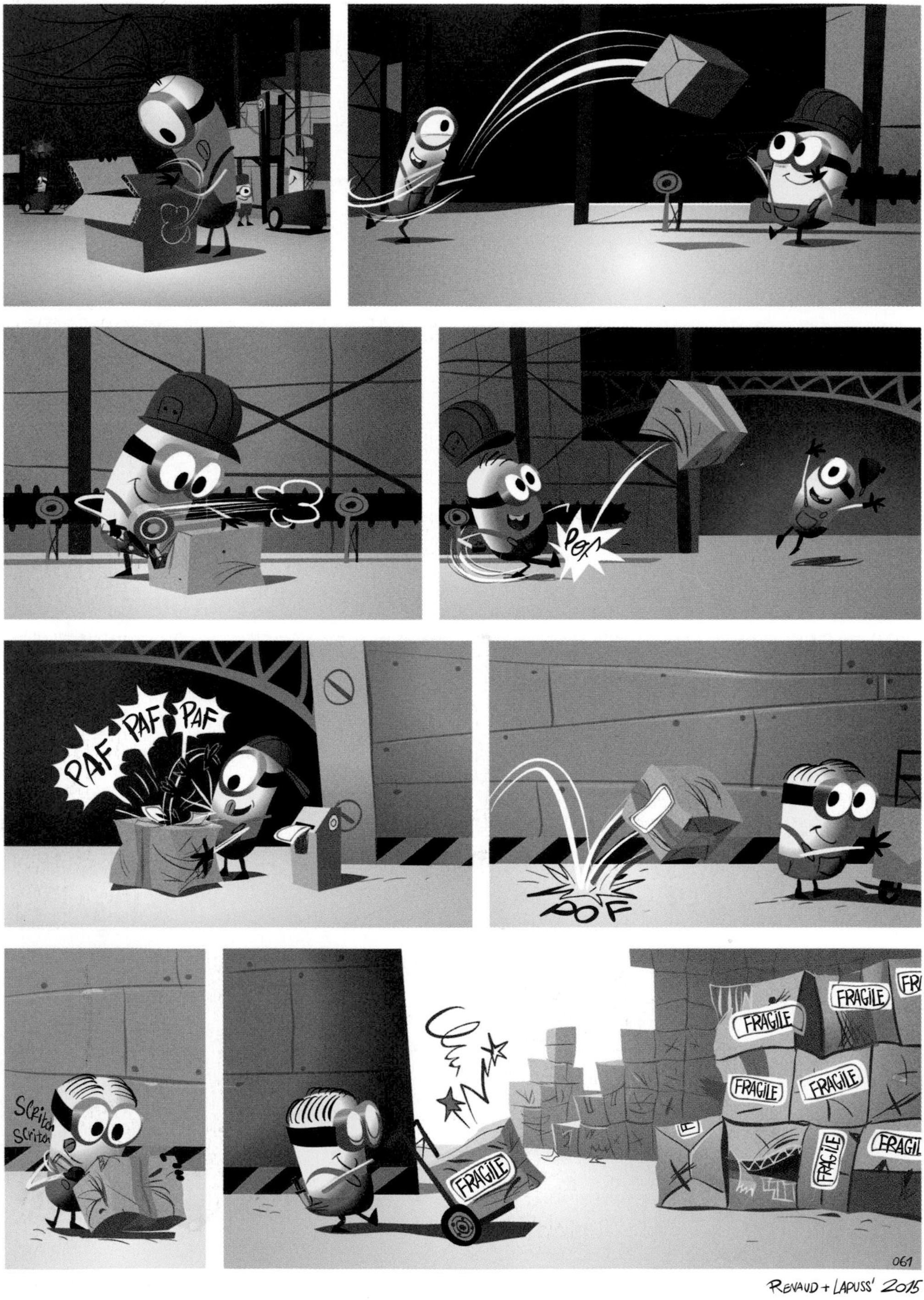
PAF
PAF
PAF
POF
SCRitch
FRAGILE
FRAGILE
FRAGILE
FRAGILE
FRAGILE
FRAGILE
FRAGILE

RENAUD + LAPUSS' 2015

FULL BACK

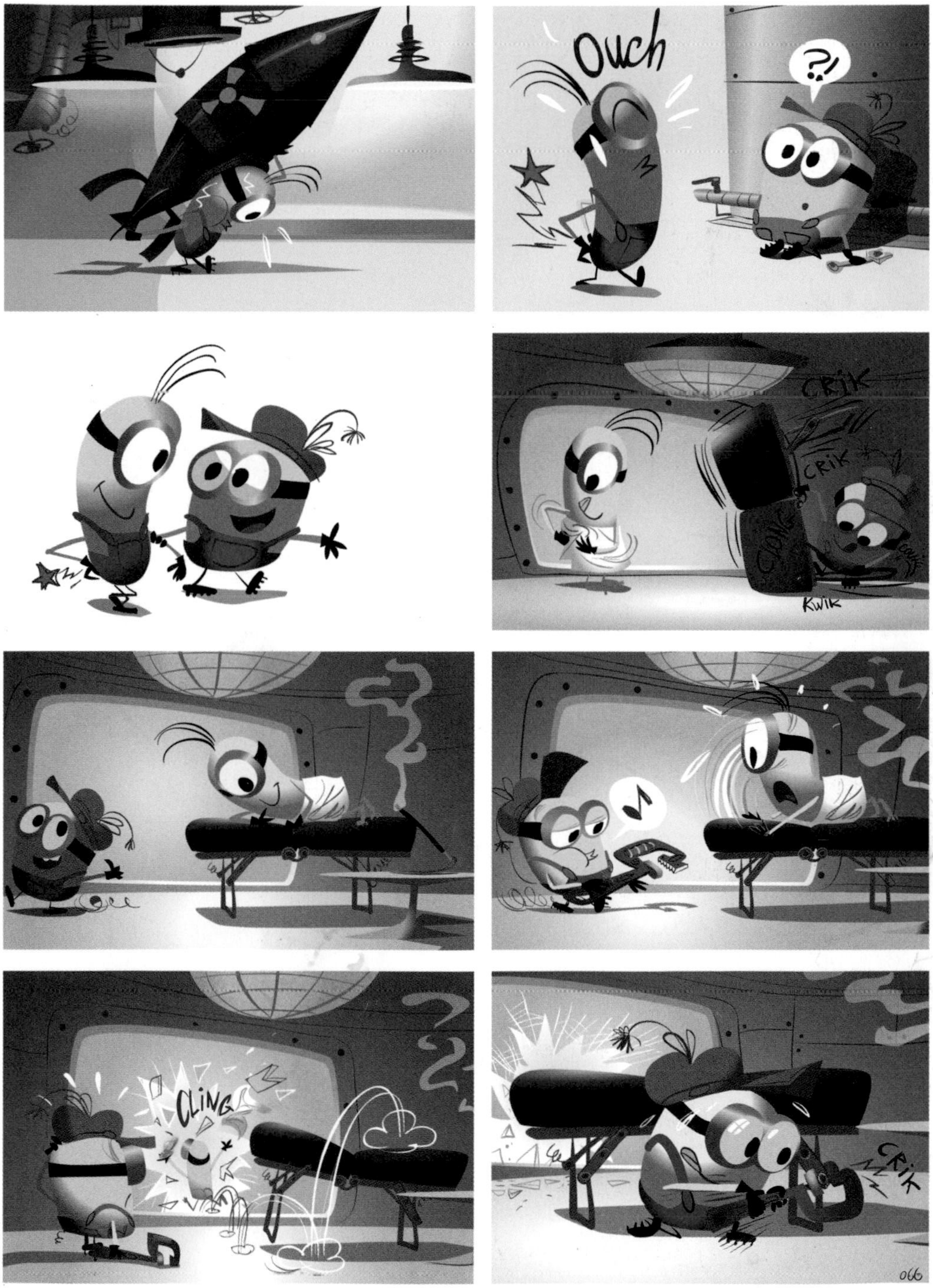
Ouch
?!
CRIK
CRIK
CLONG
KWIK
CLING
CRIK

RENAUD + LAPUSS' 2015

NO MILK TODAY

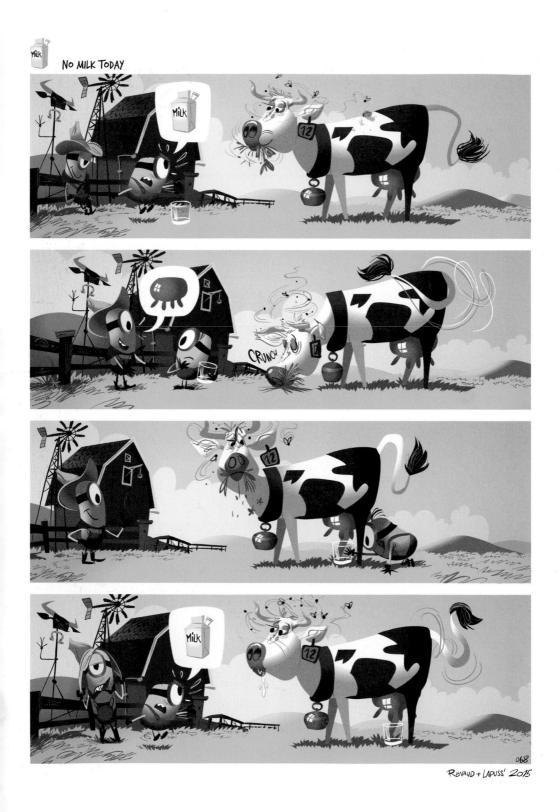

REVAUD + LAPUSS' 2015

FIRE ALARM

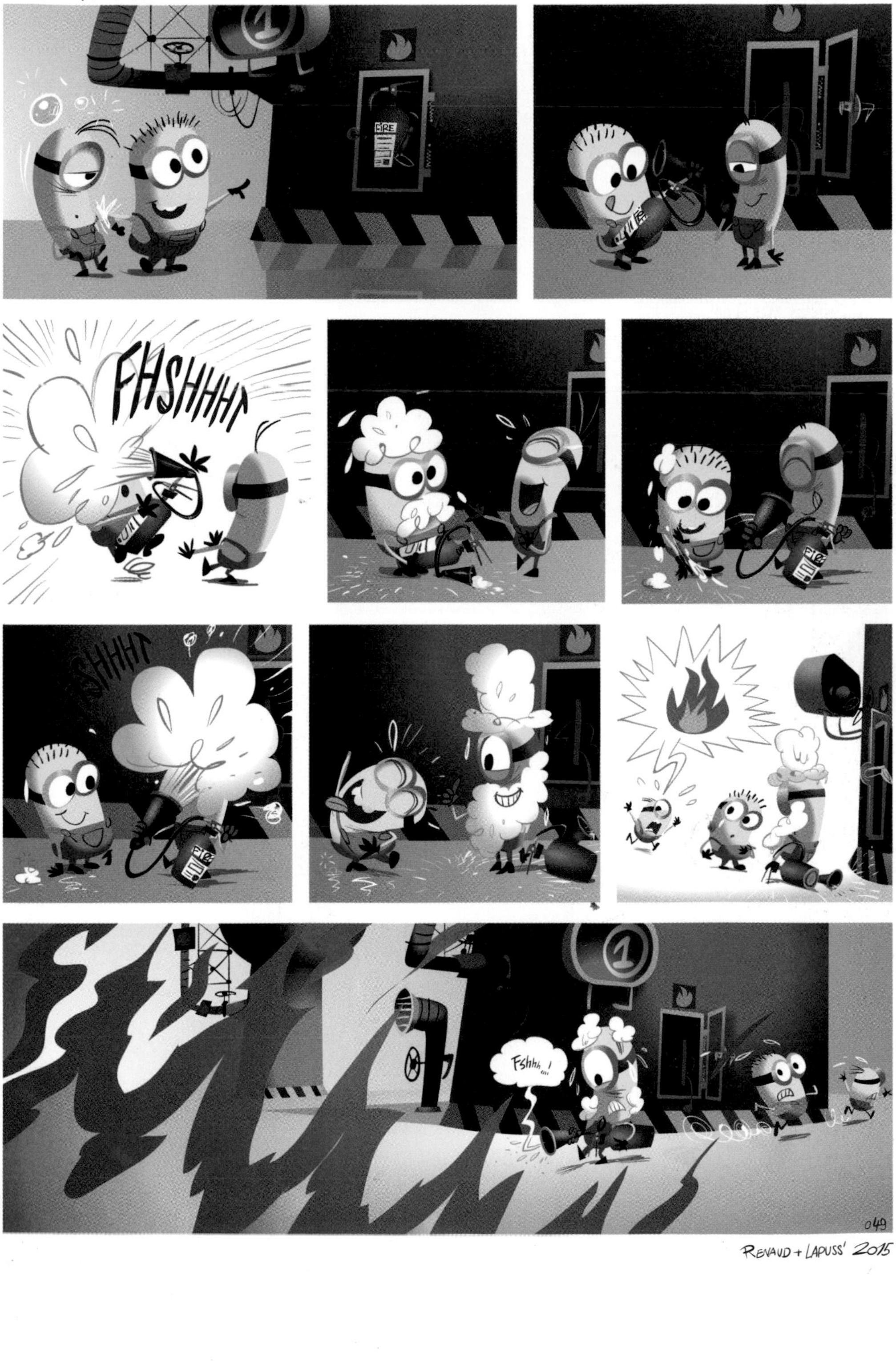
FIRE
FHSHHHT
SHHHT
Fshhh..!

RENAUD + LAPUSS' 2015

BANANAAAH !

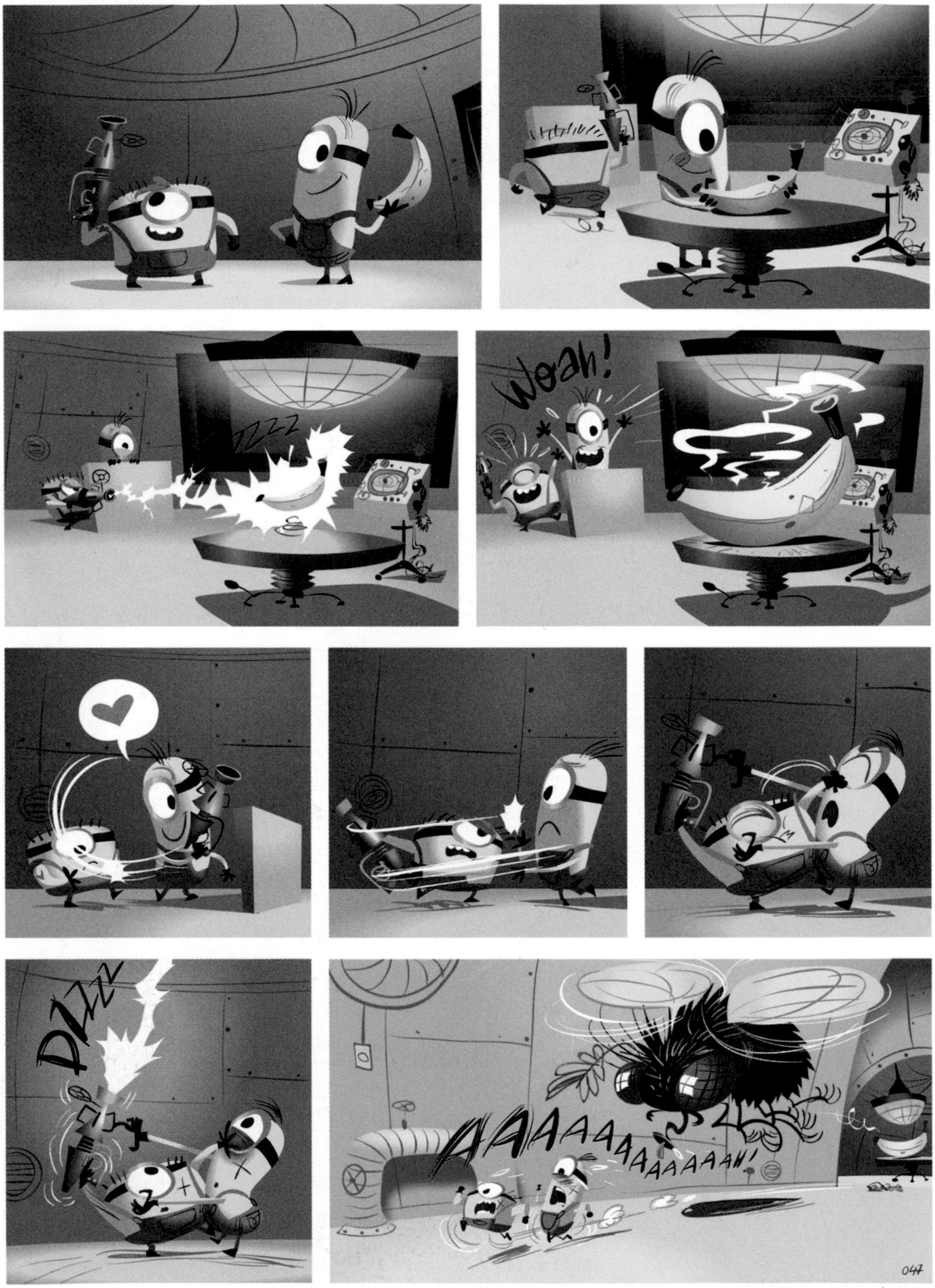
ZZZZ
Woah!
DZZz
AAAAAAAAAAAAAH!

RENAUD + LAPUSS' 2015

ICE CREAM 1

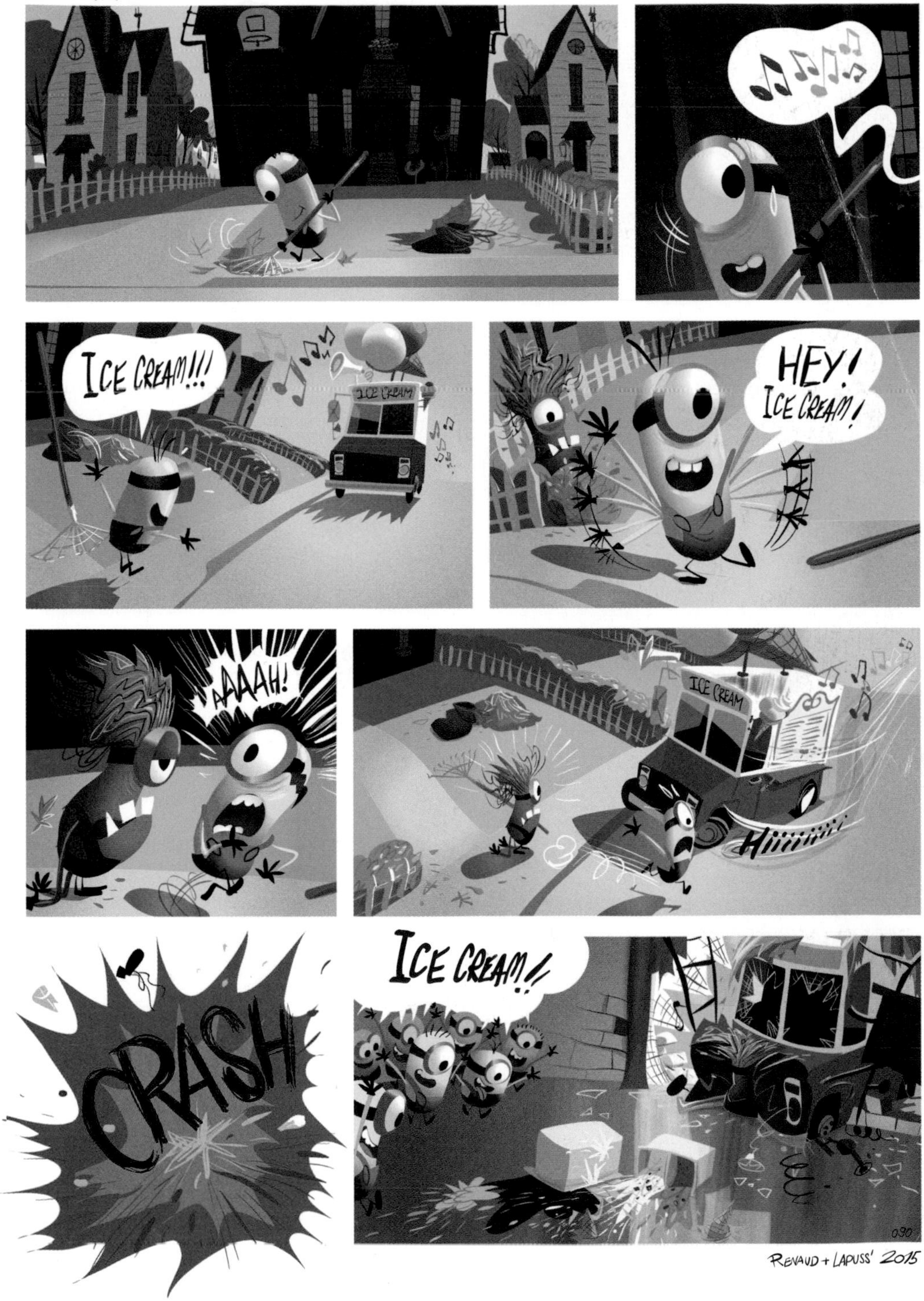
ICE CREAM!!!
ICE CREAM
HEY!
ICE CREAM!
AAAAH!
ICE CREAM
Hiiiiiiii
CRASH
ICE CREAM!!

RENAUD + LAPUSS' 2015

CHERRY ON THE CAKE

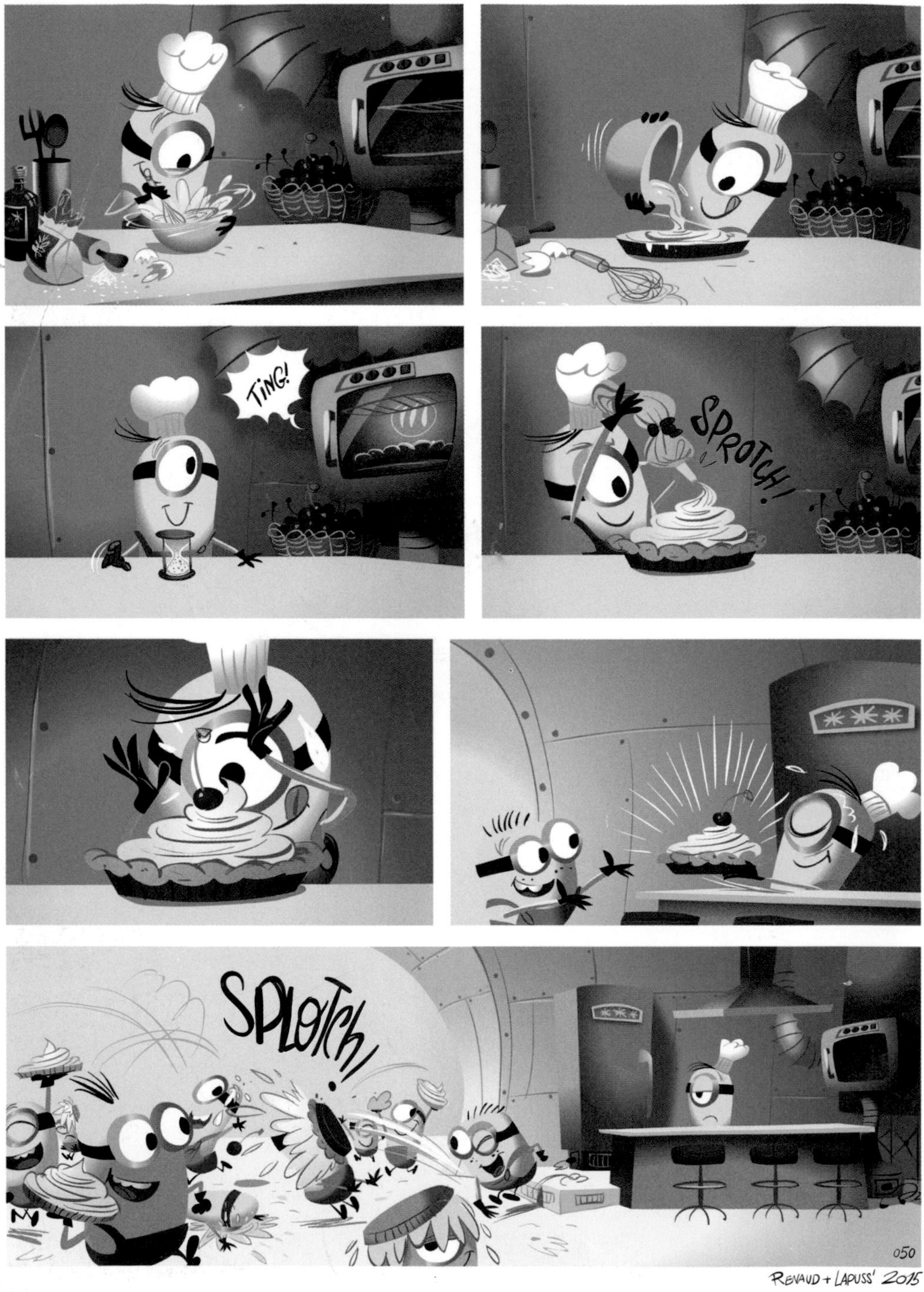
TING!
SPROTCH!
SPLOTCH!
050

RENAUD + LAPUSS' 2015

THE HEAT IS ON!

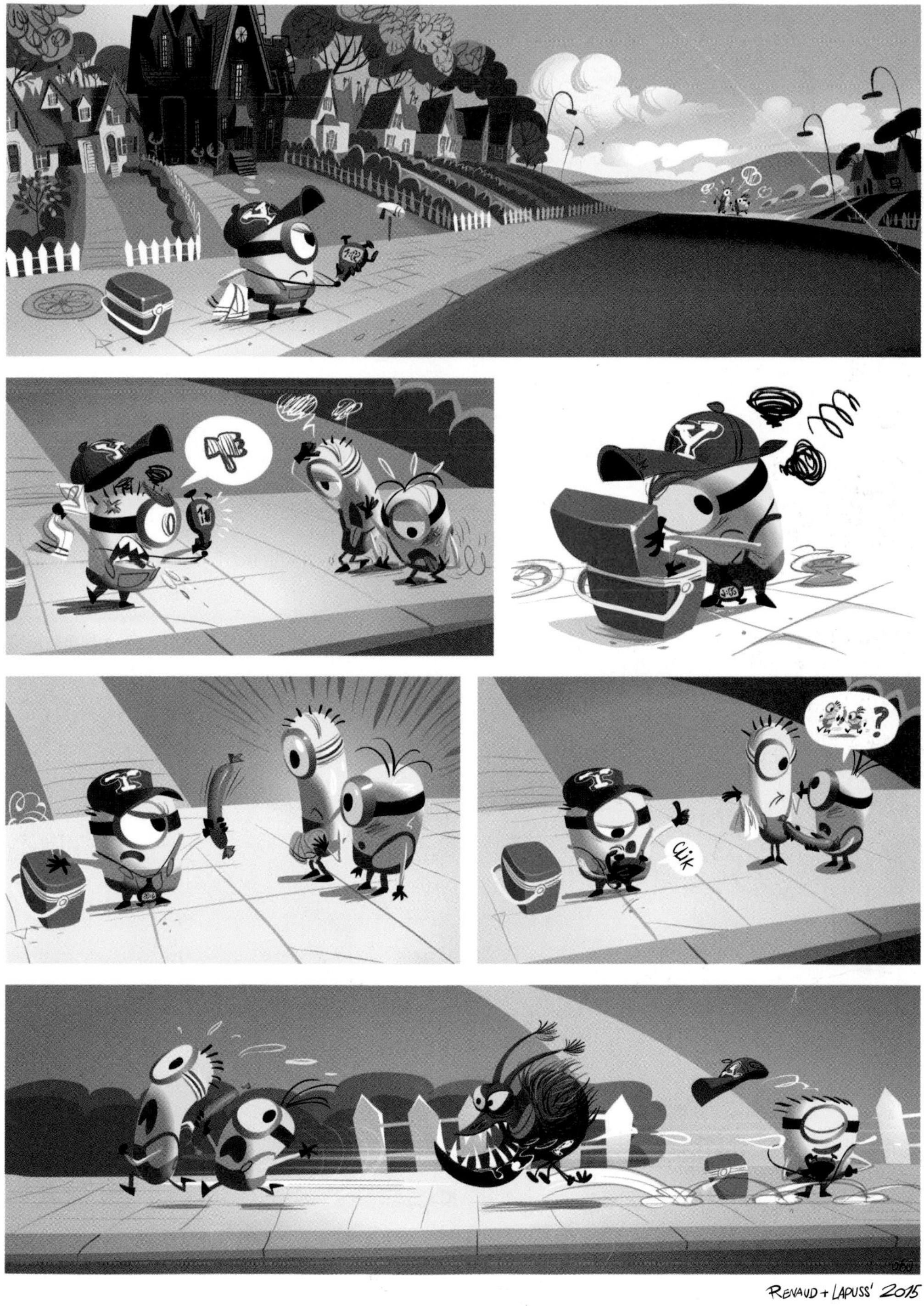
CLIK

RENAUD + LAPUSS' 2015

PIGGY BANK

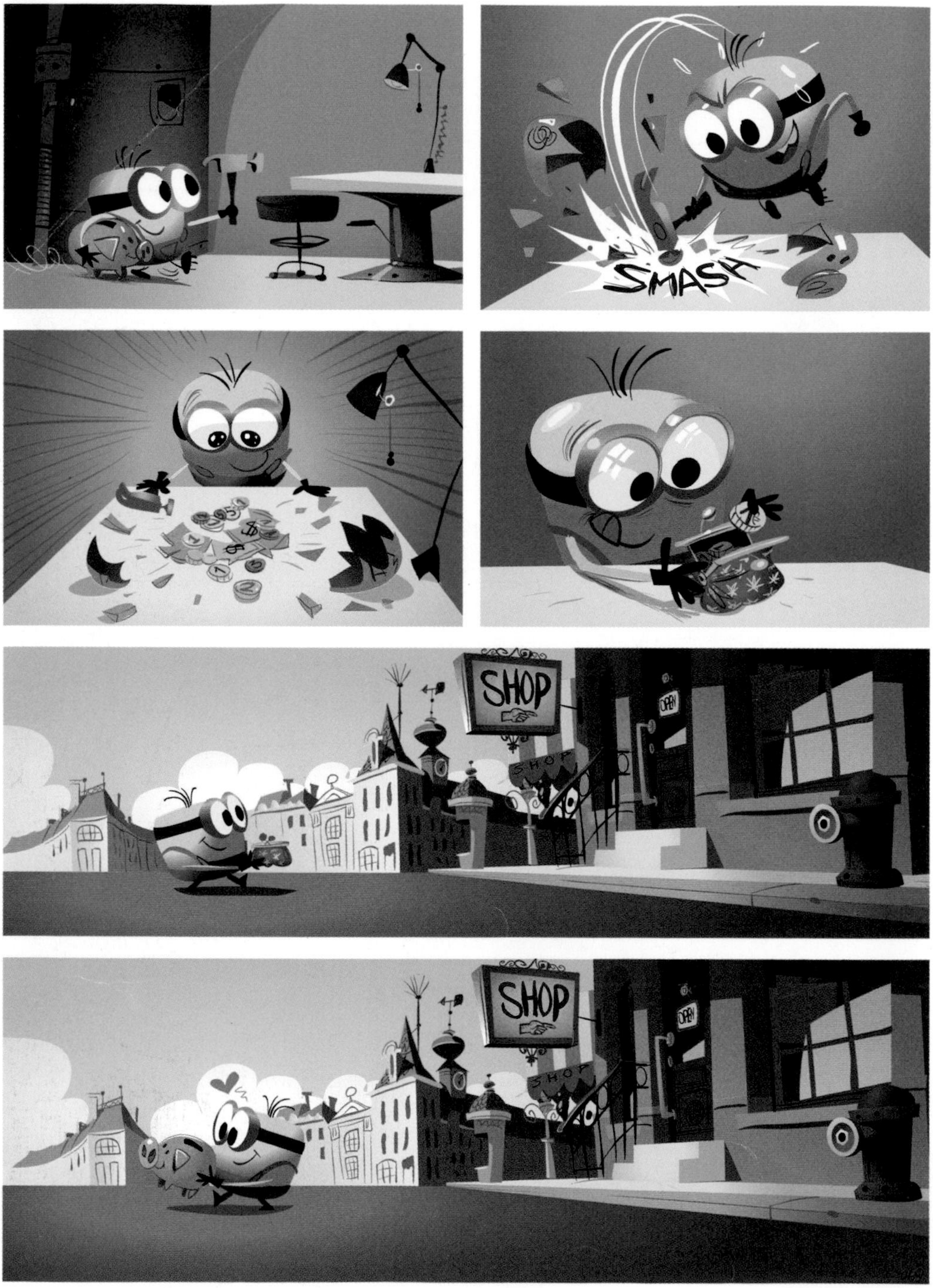
SMASH
SHOP
OPEN
SHOP
SHOP
OPEN
SHOP

RENAUD + LAPUSS' 2015

STILL LIFE

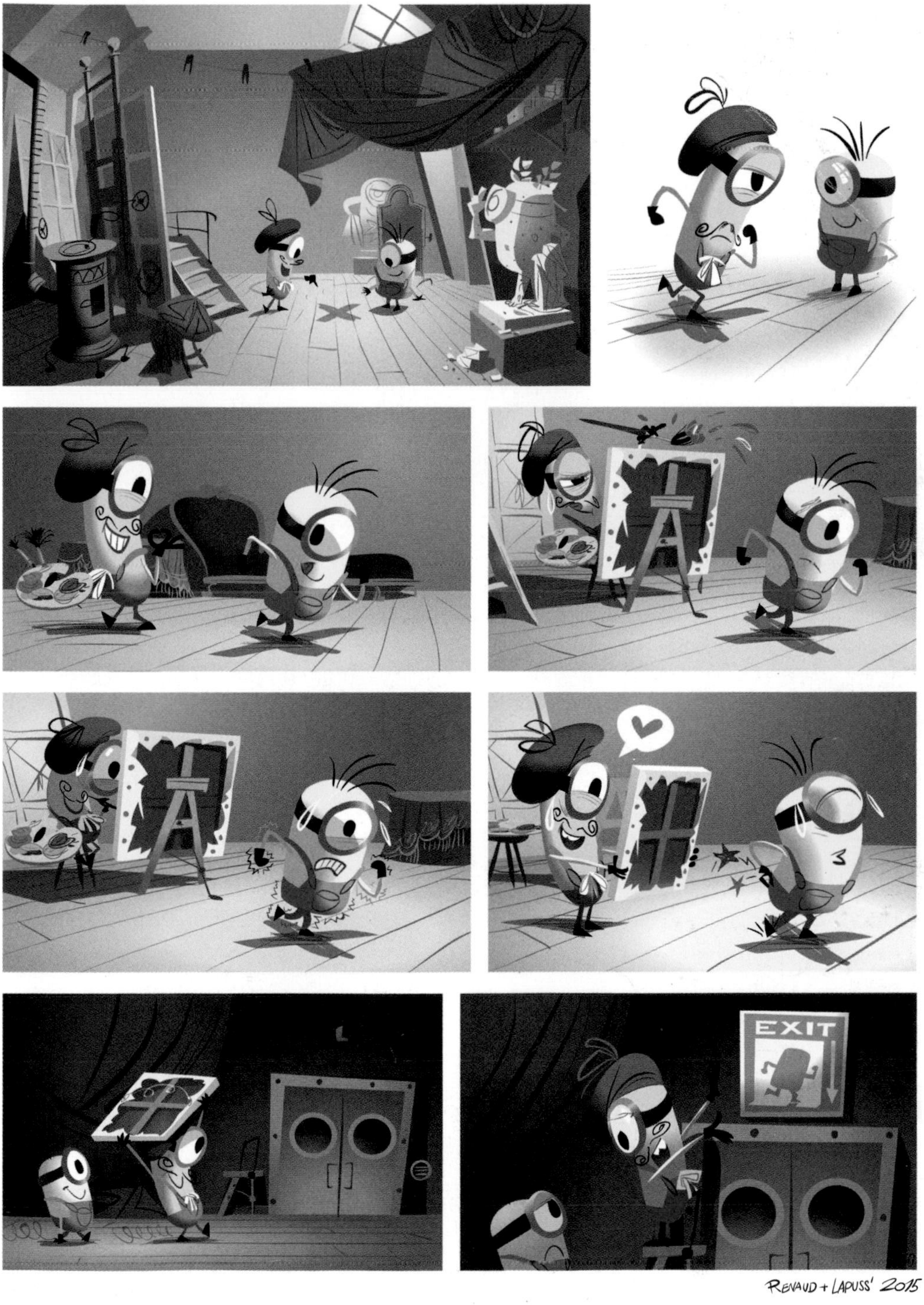
EXIT

RENAUD + LAPUSS' 2015

COFFEE BREAK

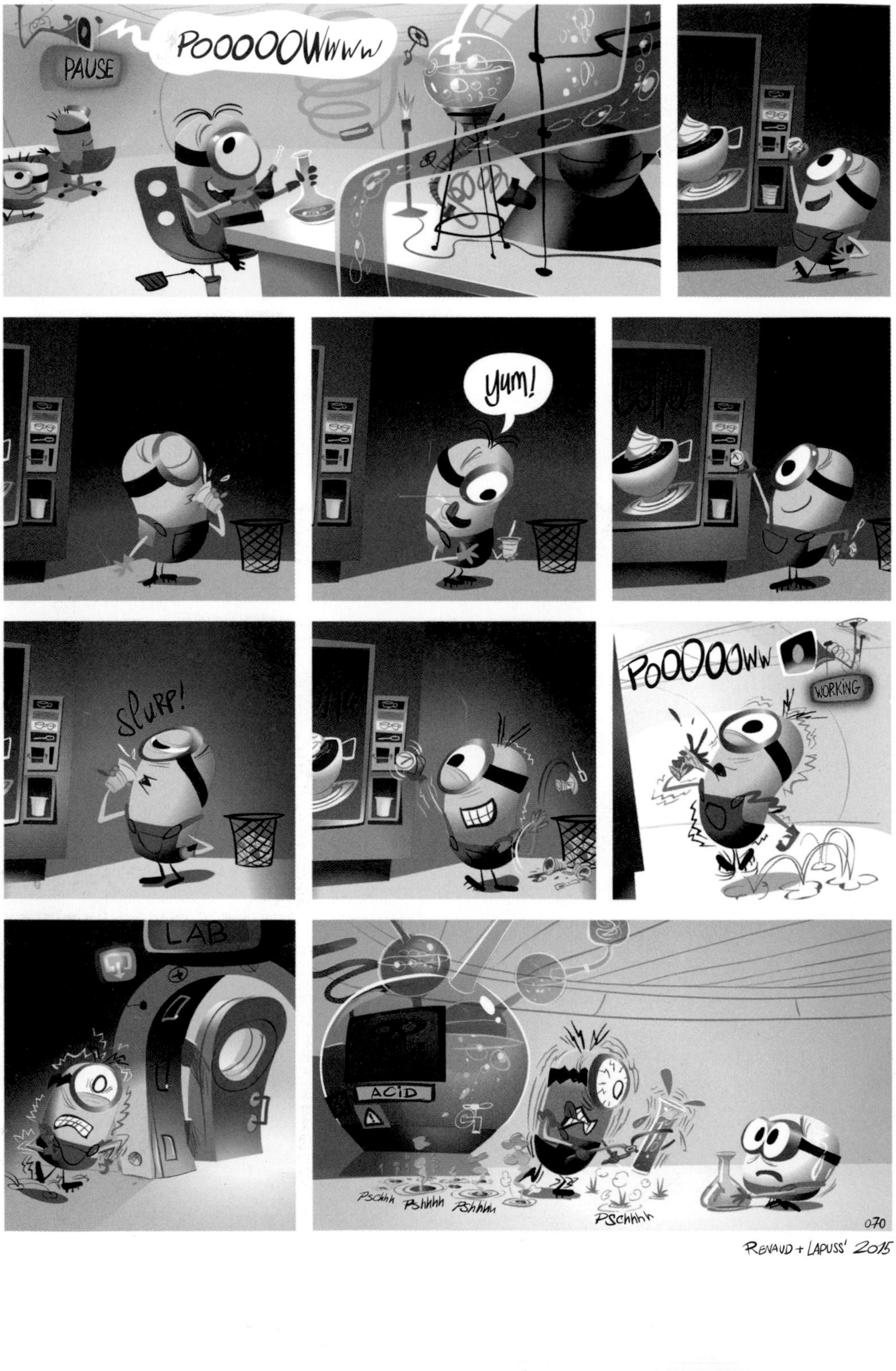
PAUSE
POOOOOWwww
Yum!
Slurp!
POOOOOWW
WORKING
LAB
ACID
Pschhh
Pshhhh
Pshhhh
PSchhhh

RENAUD + LAPUSS' 2015

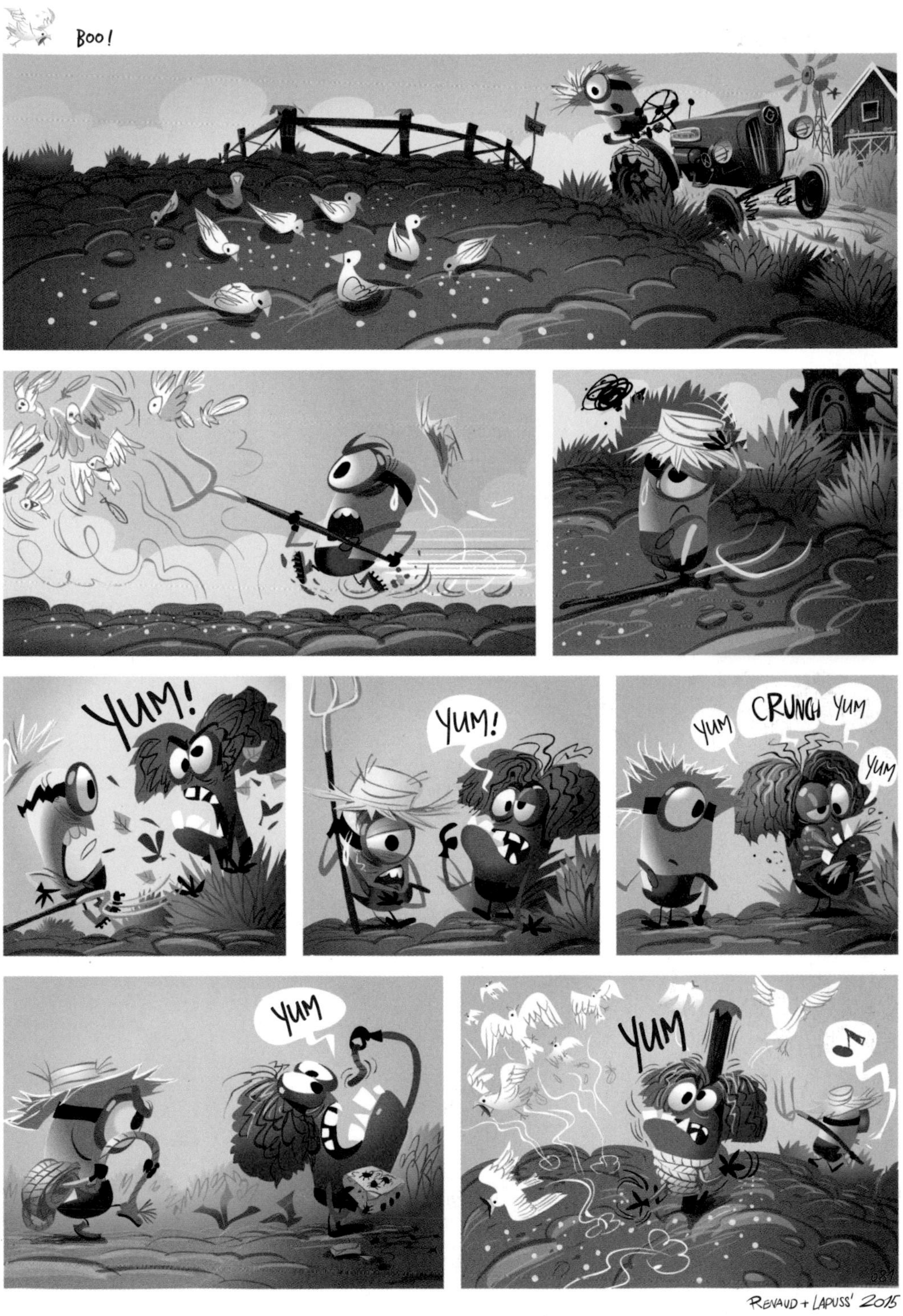
Boo!
YUM!
YUM!
YUM
CRUNCH
YUM
YUM
YUM
YUM

RENAUD + LAPUSS' 2015

KING OF THE RING

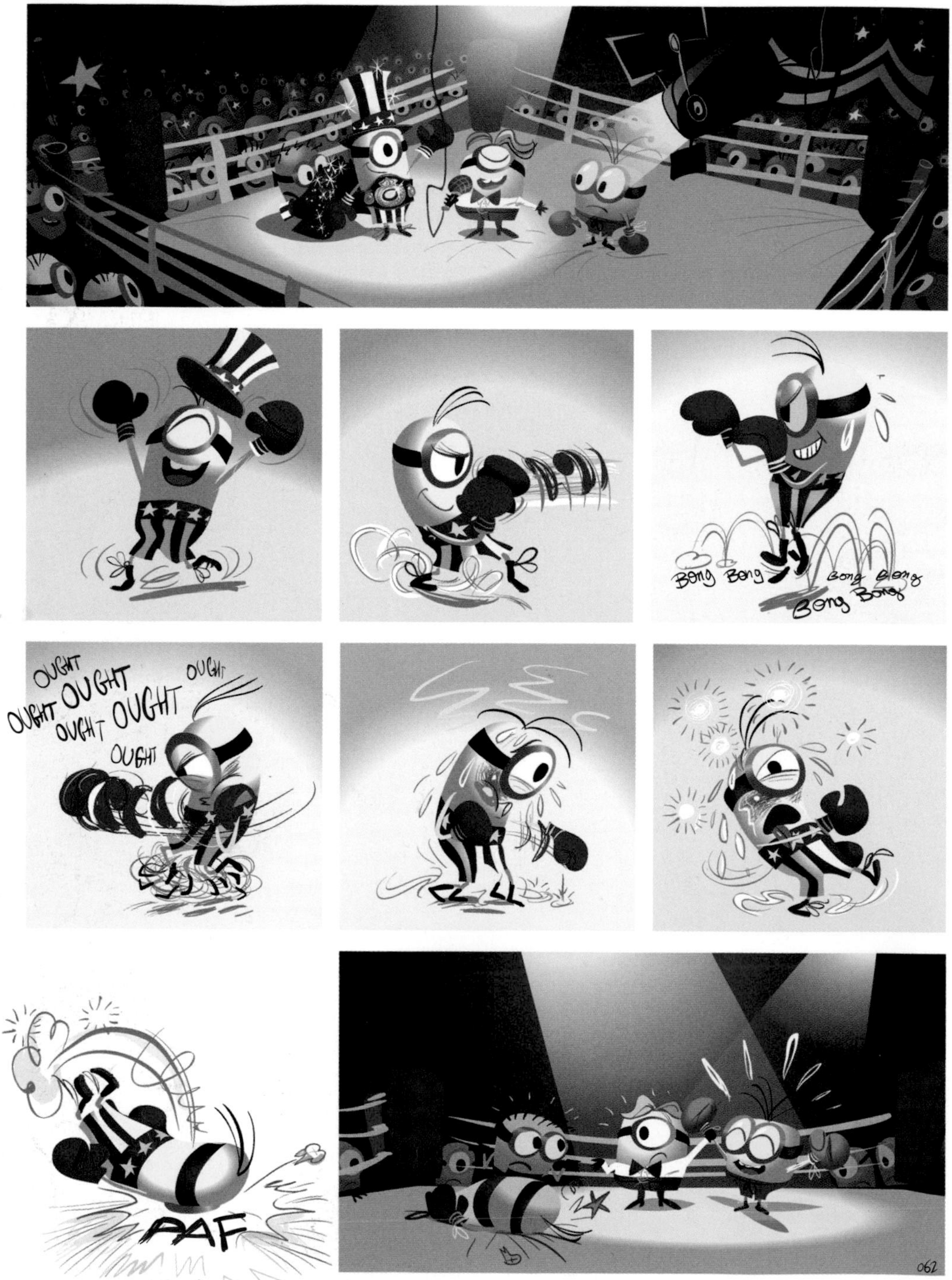
Bong Bong
Bong Bong
Bong Bong
OUGHT
OUGHT OUGHT
OUGHT
OUGHT OUGHT
OUGHT
PAF

RENAUD + LAPUSS' 2015

ICE CREAM II

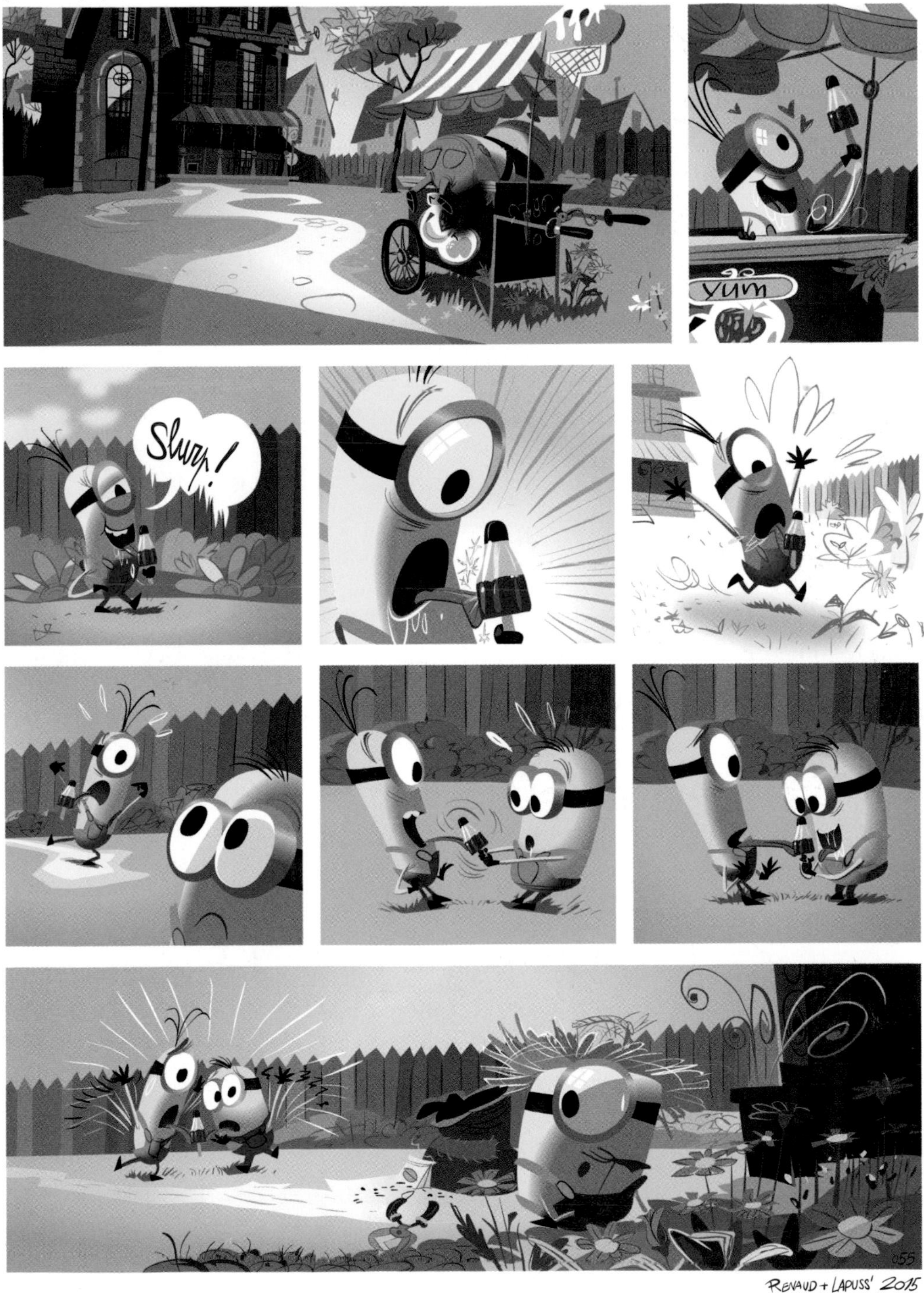
YUM
Slurp!
055

RENAUD + LAPUSS' 2015

ROCK ATTITUDE

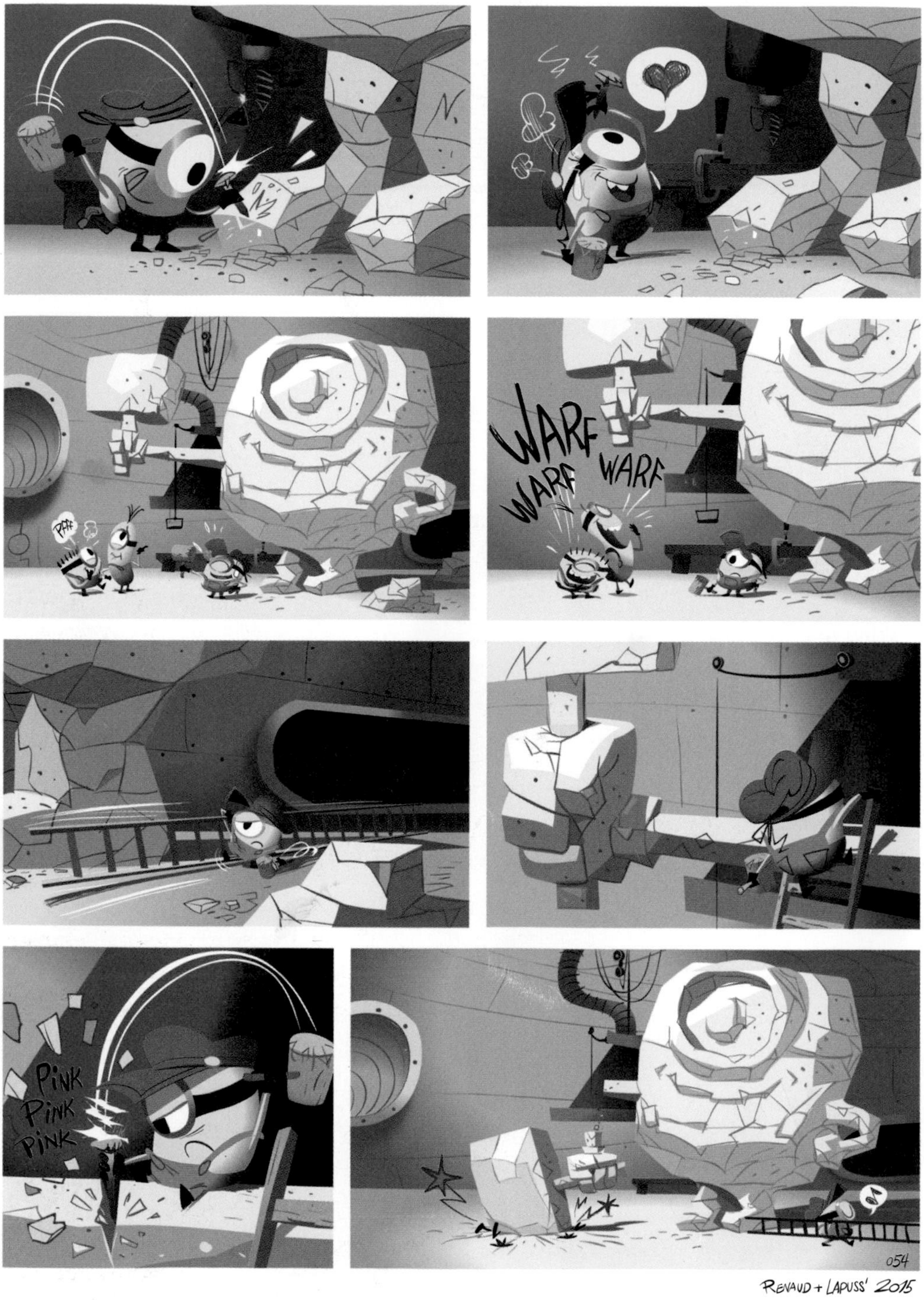
WARF
WARF
WARF
WARF
PINK
PINK
PINK

RENAUD + LAPUSS' 2015

BANANA BAR

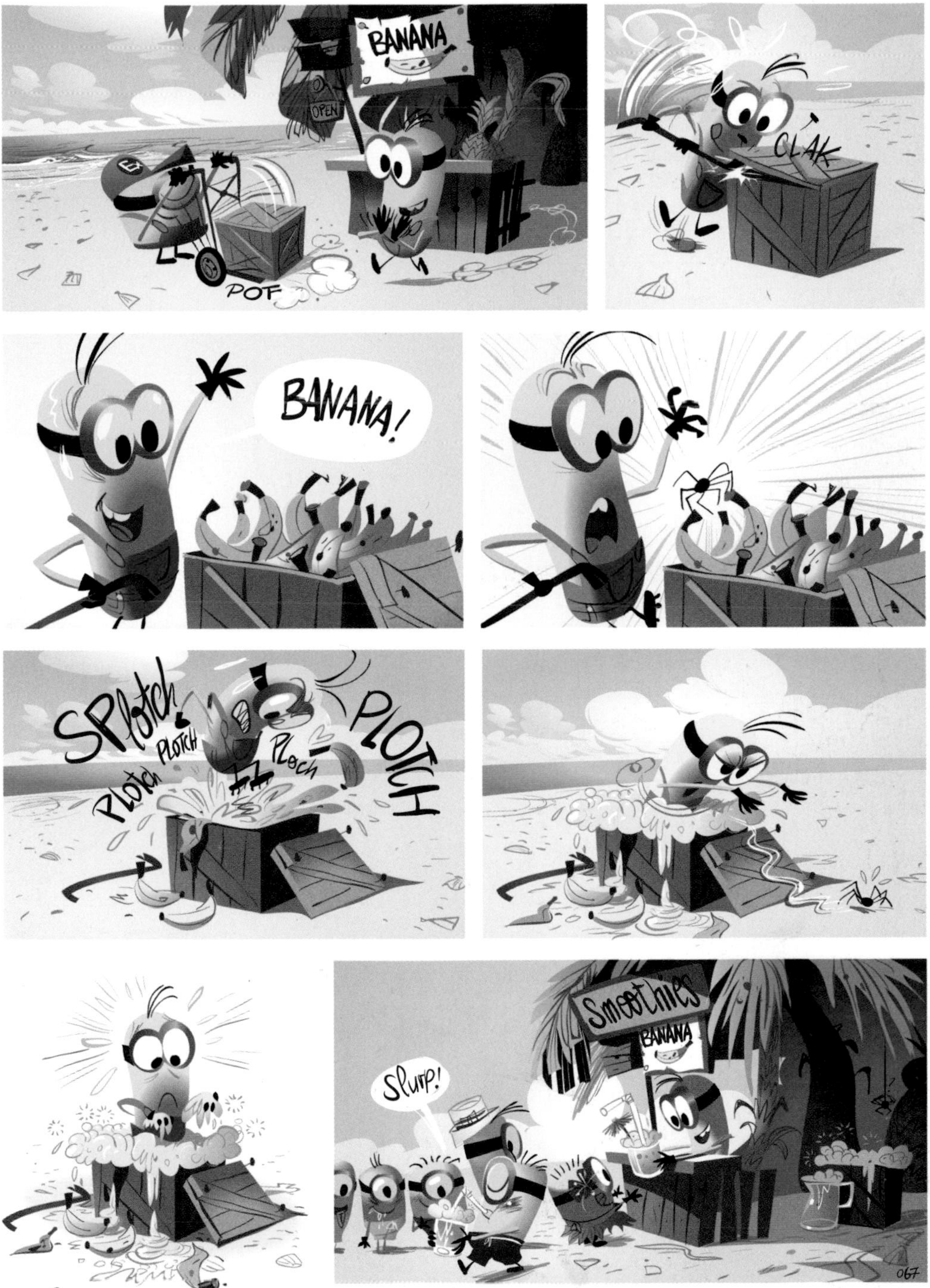
BANANA
OPEN
POF
CLAK
BANANA!
SPlotch
PLOTCH
Plotch
Plech
PLOTCH
Smoothies
BANANA
Slurp!
067

RENAUD + LAPUSS' 2015

HEADPHONE ATTACK

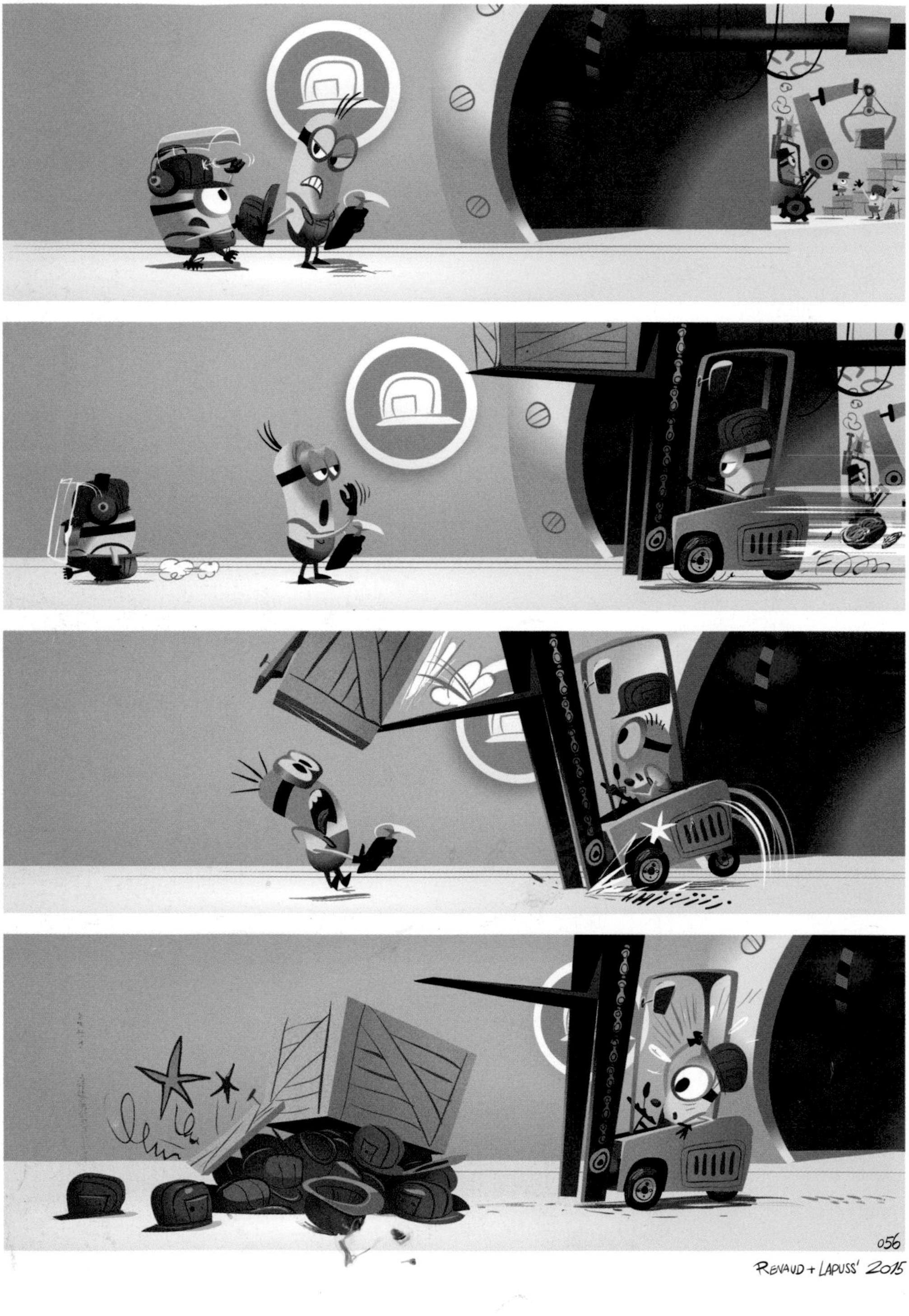

056

RENAUD + LAPUSS' 2015

EXPRESS STORAGE

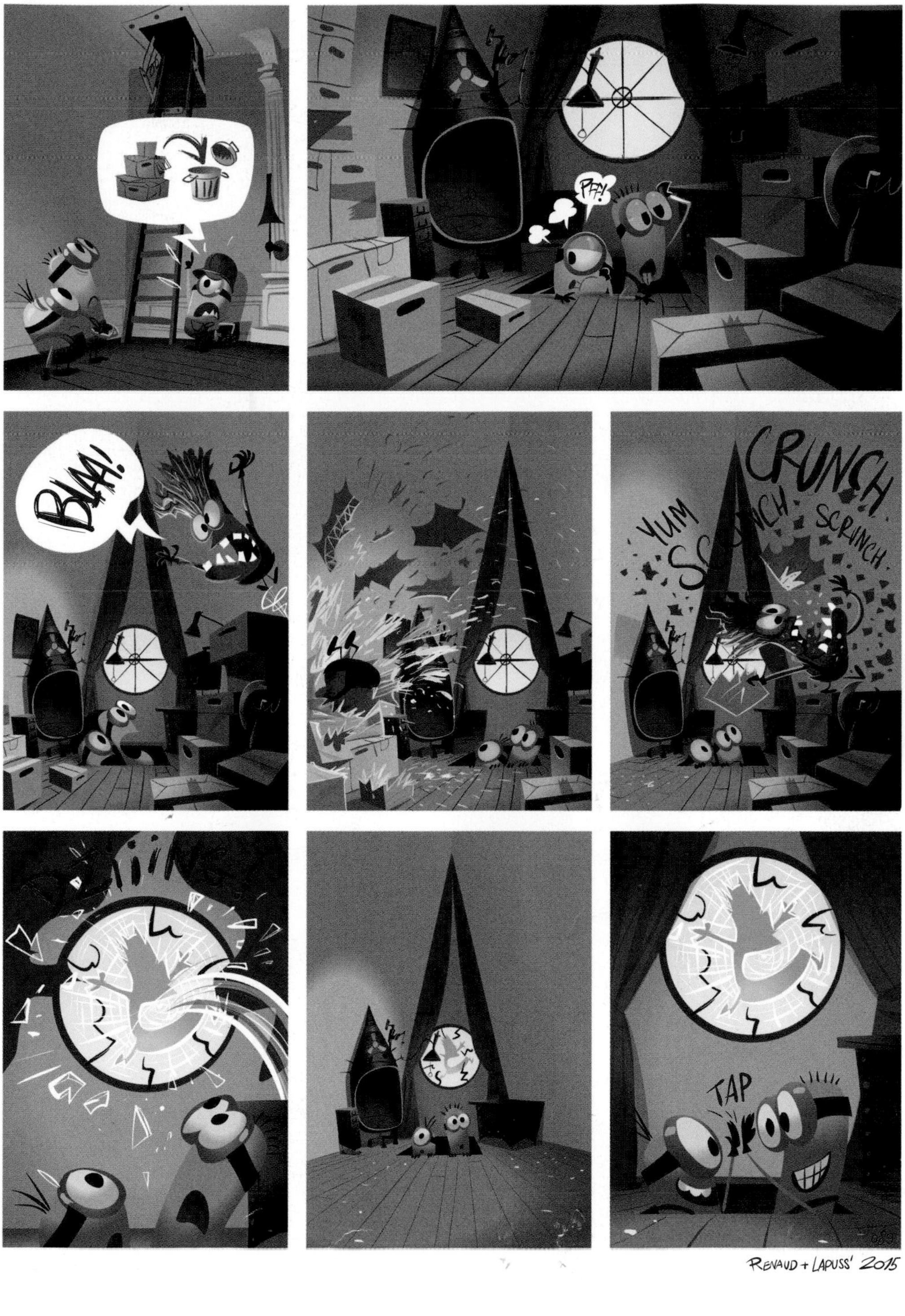
PFF!
BLAA!
CRUNCH
YUM
SCRUNCH
SCRUNCH
TAP

RENAUD + LAPUSS' 2015

DRY CLEANING

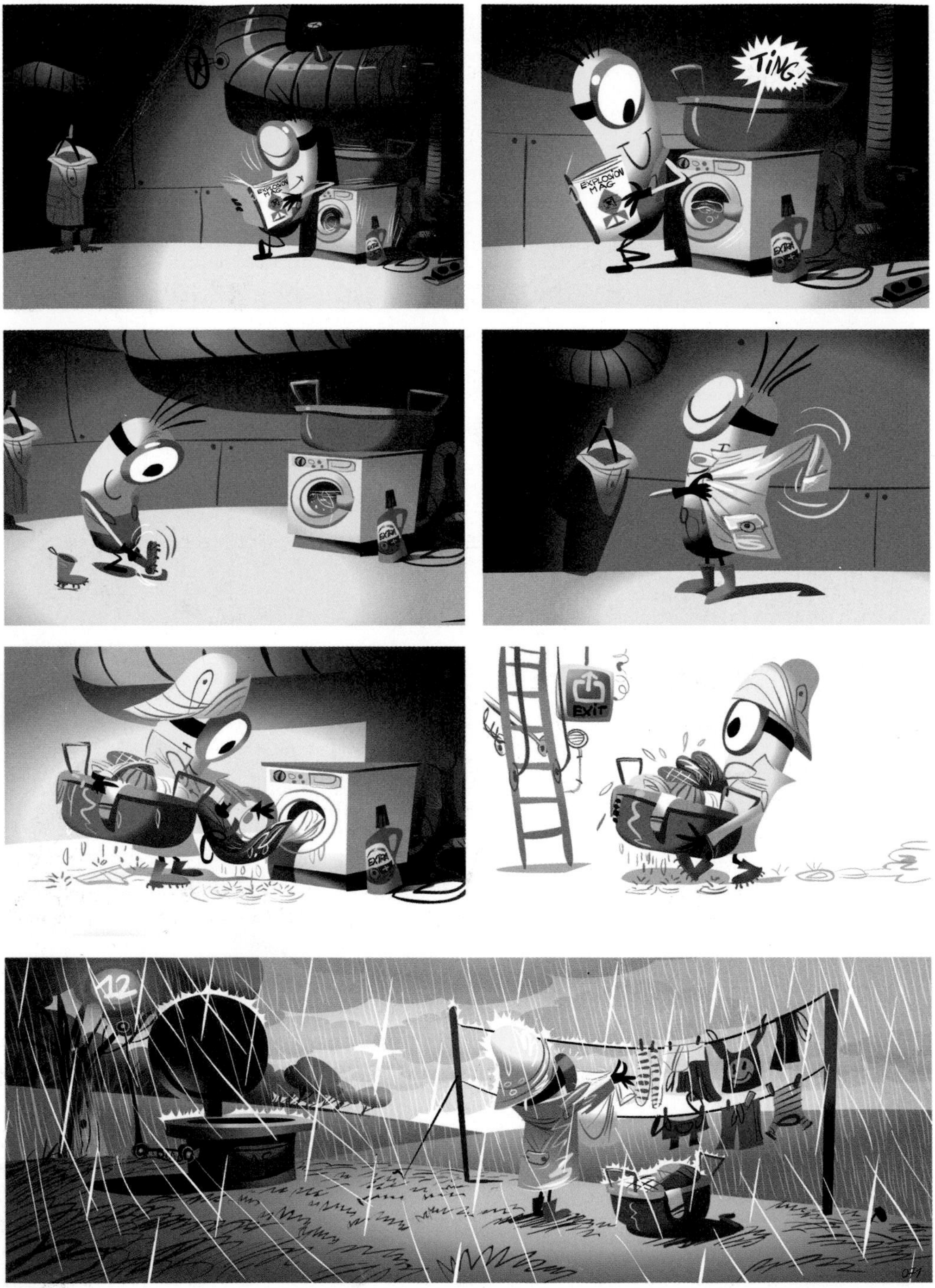
EXPLOSION MAG
TING!
EXPLOSION MAG
EXTRA
EXIT
12

RENAUD + LAPUSS' 2015

THE SAUCE

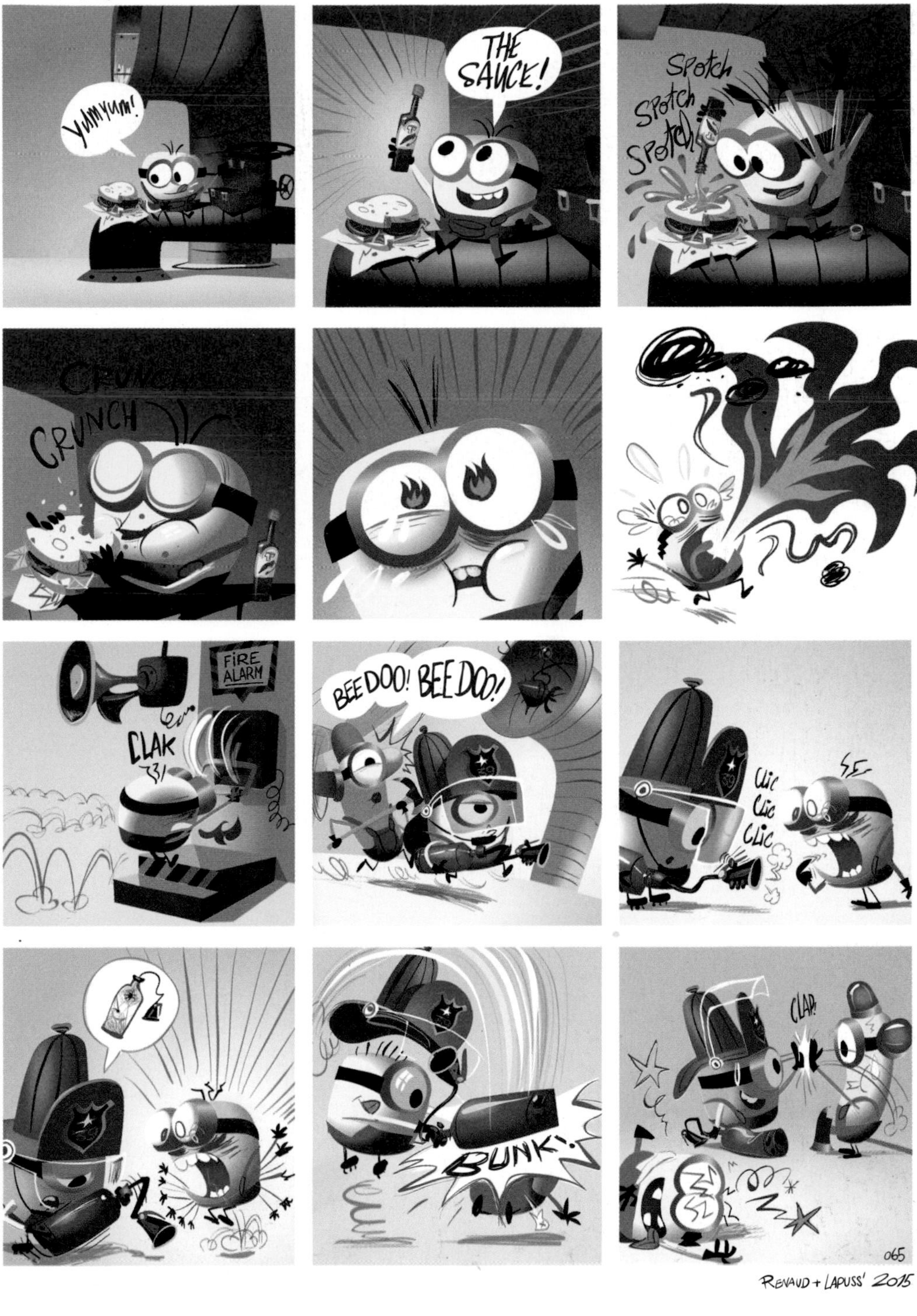

YUMYUM!
THE SAUCE!
SPOTCH
SPOTCH
SPOTCH
CRUNCH
CRUNCH
FIRE ALARM
CLAK
BEEDOO! BEEDOO!
CLIC
CLIC
CLIC
BUNK!
CLAP!

RENAUD + LAPUSS' 2015

WHAT'S HOT!

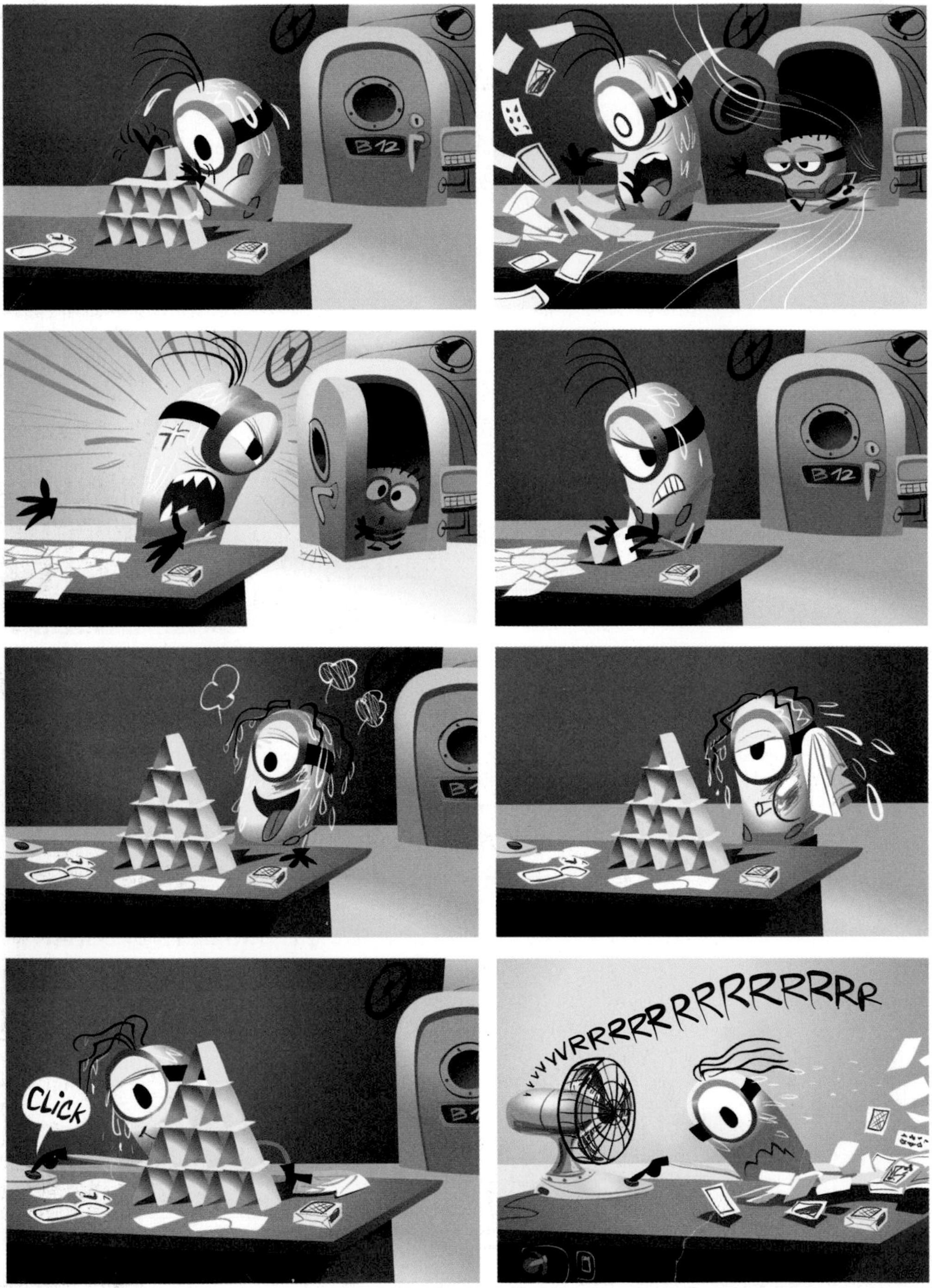
B 12
CLICK
vvvvvVRRRRRRRRRRRRR

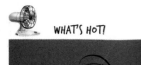

RENAUD + LAPUSS' 2015

MEXICO

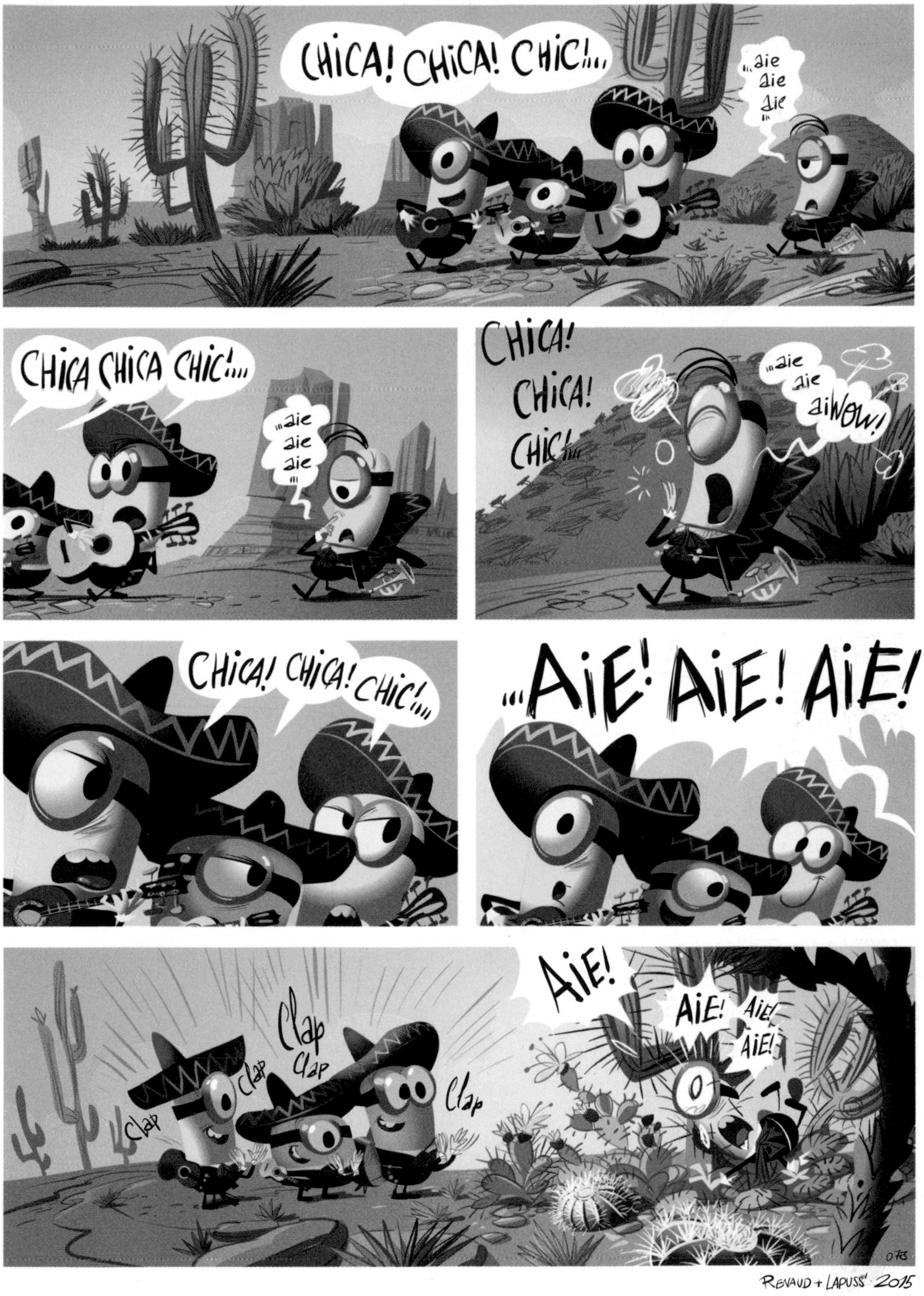
CHICA! CHICA! CHIC!...
...aie aie aie ..
CHICA CHICA CHIC!...
...aie aie aie ...
CHICA! CHICA! CHIC!...
...aie aie aiWOW!
CHICA! CHICA! CHIC!...
...AIE! AIE! AIE!
Clap Clap Clap Clap Clap
AIE!
AIE! AIE! AIE!

RENAUD + LAPUSS' 2015

DOUBLE PICKLES

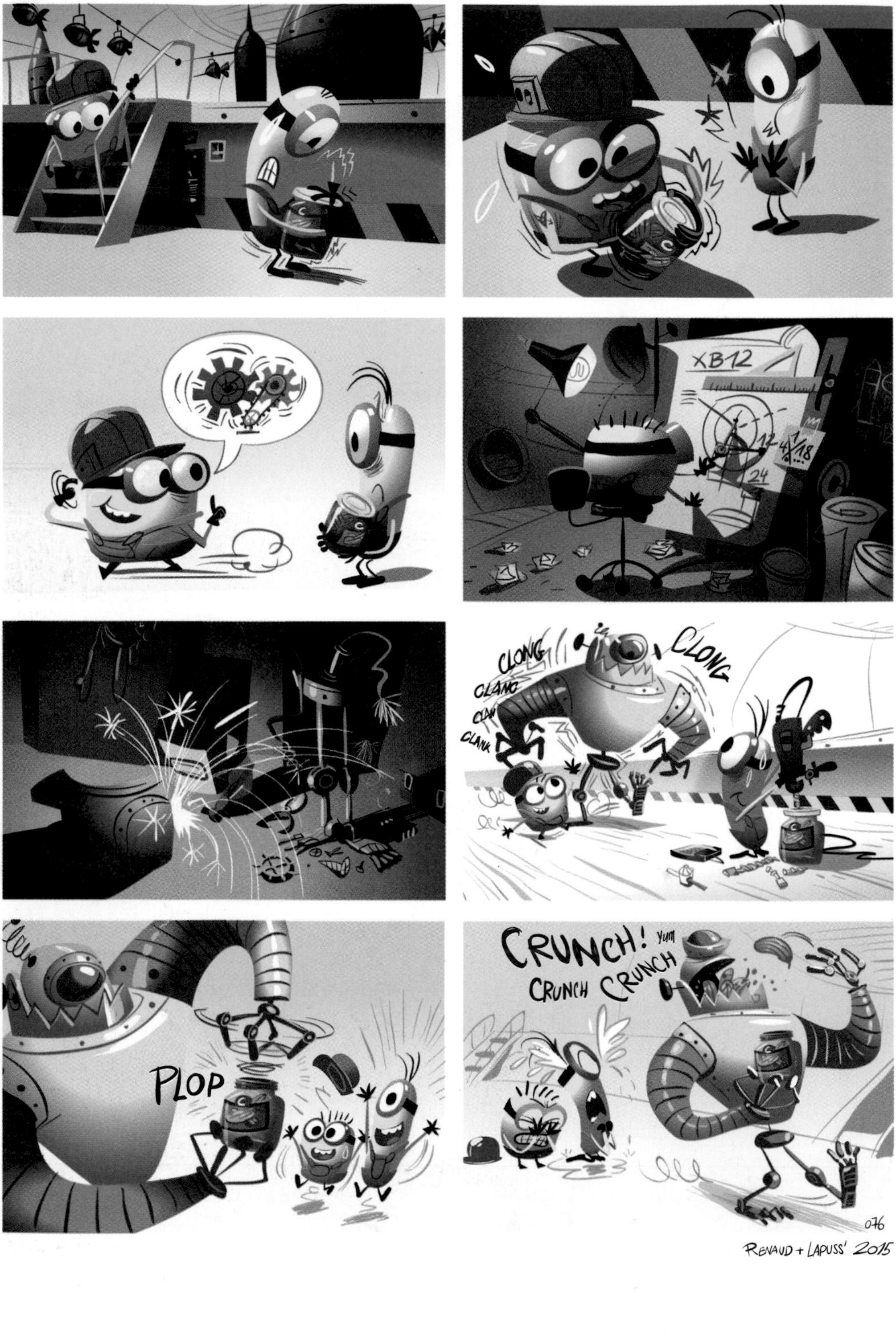
XB12
CLONG
CLONG
CLANG
CLANK
PLOP
CRUNCH! yum
CRUNCH CRUNCH

RENAUD + LAPUSS' 2015

GREEDY

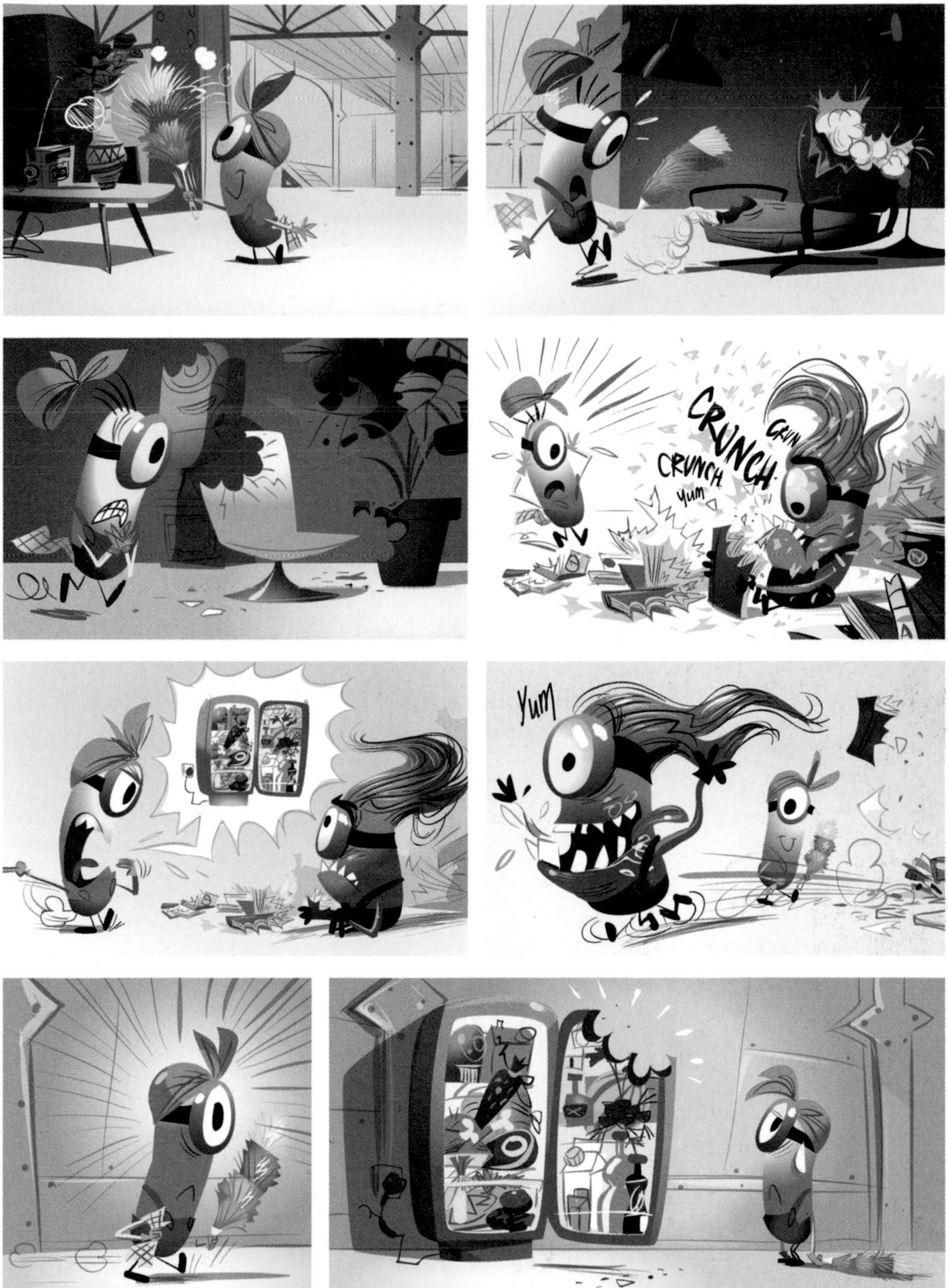

CRUNCH
GRUN
CRUNCH
yum
Yum

RENAUD + LAPUSS' 2015

CHINESE SHADOWS

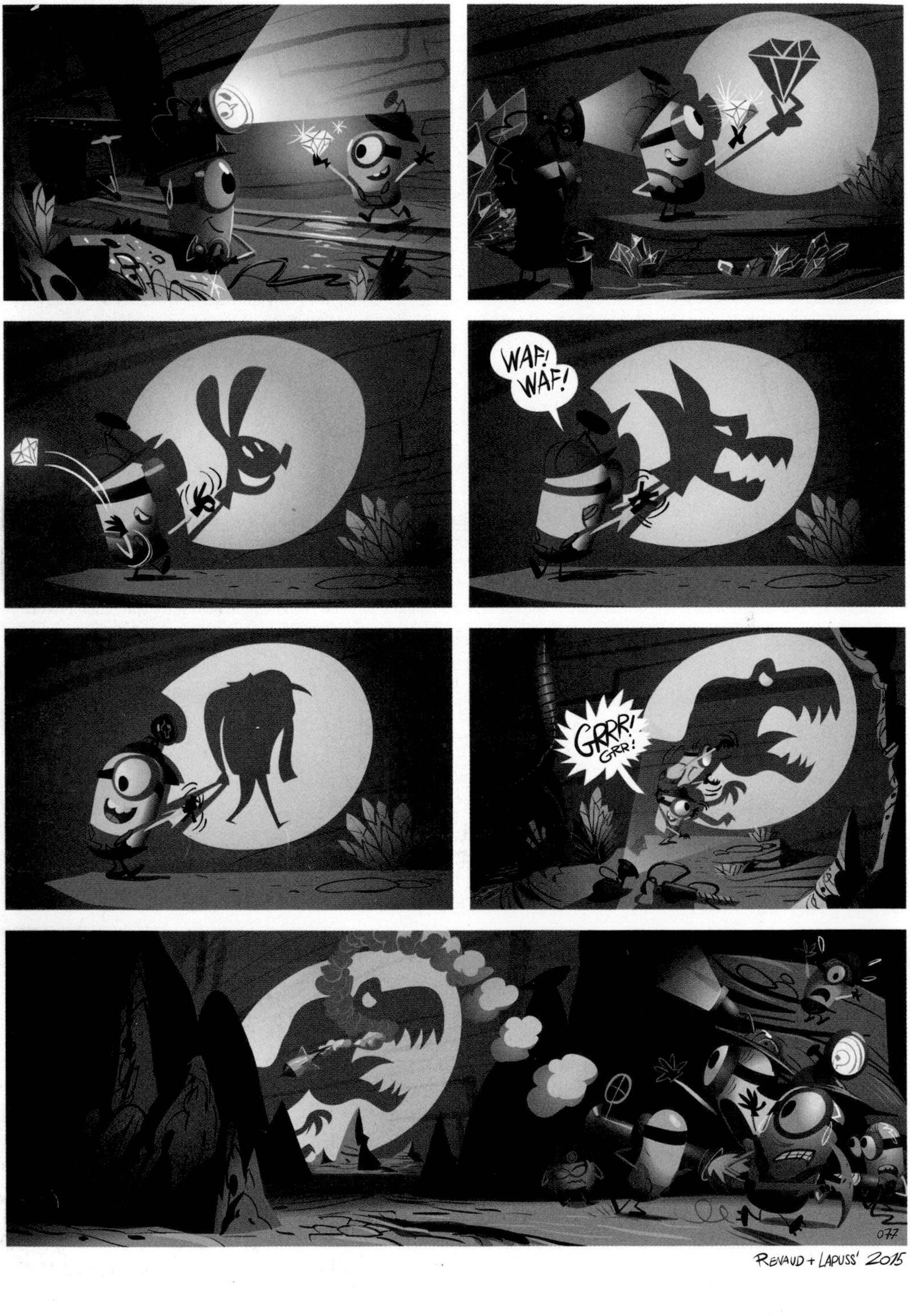
WAF! WAF!
GRRR! GRR!
077

RENAUD + LAPUSS' 2015

FLOWER POWER

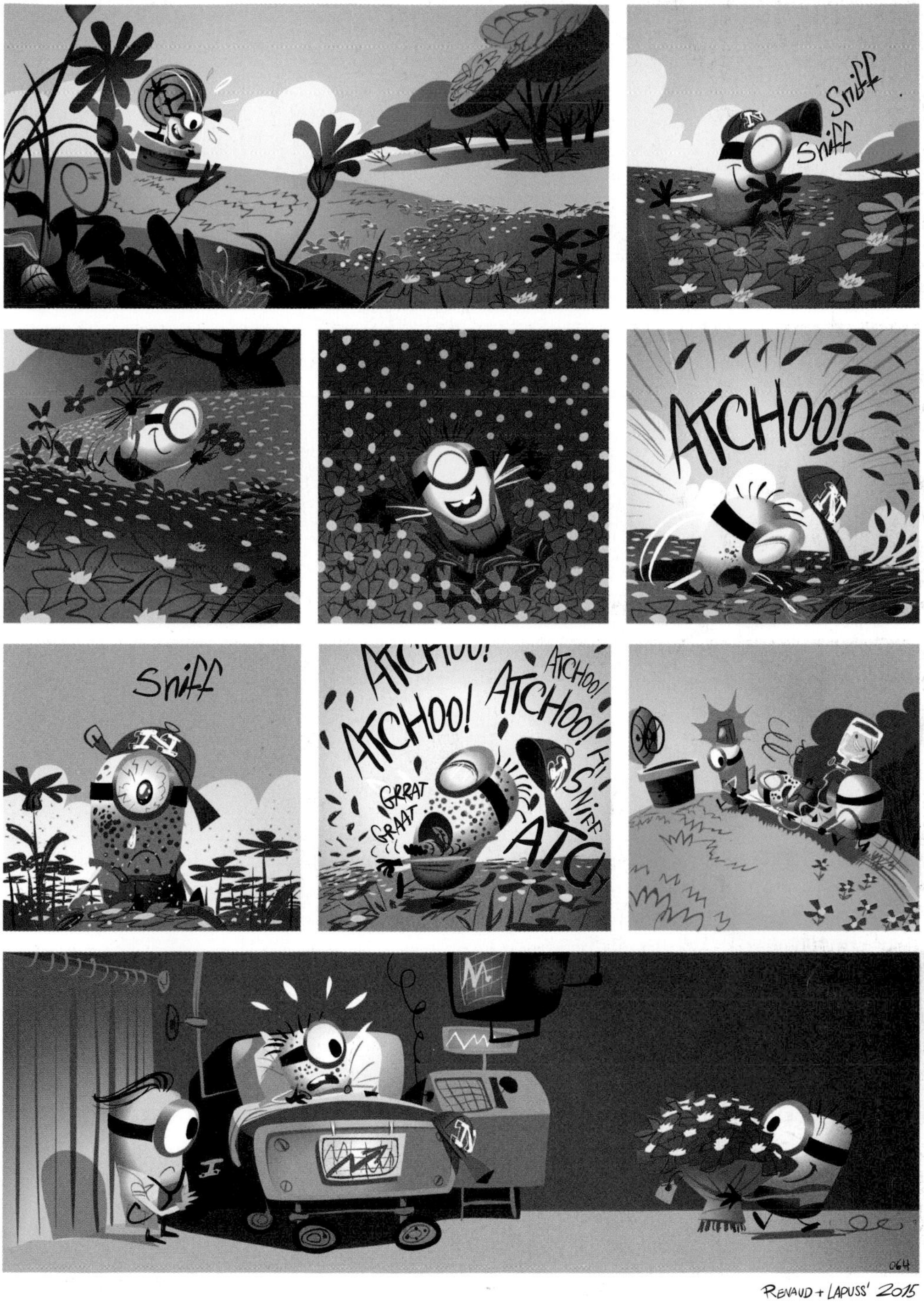

Sniff
Sniff
ATCHOO!
Sniff
ATCHOO!
ATCHOO!
ATCHOO!
GRRAT
GRAAT
Hi!
SNIFF

RENAUD + LAPUSS' 2015

EVIL BASKET

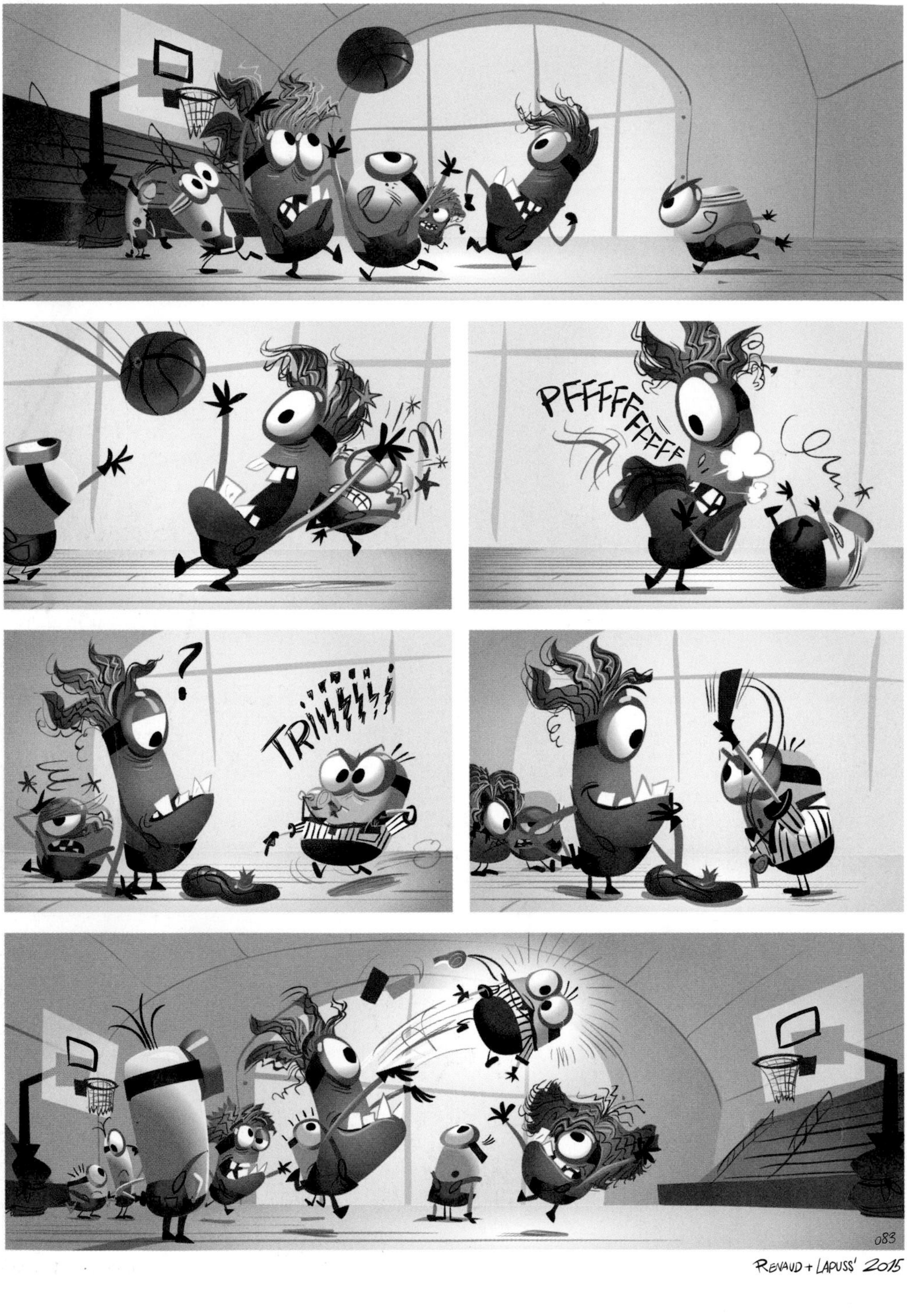
PFFFFFFFFFFF
?
TRIIIIII!

RENAUD + LAPUSS' 2015

LET'S GO TO THE BEACH

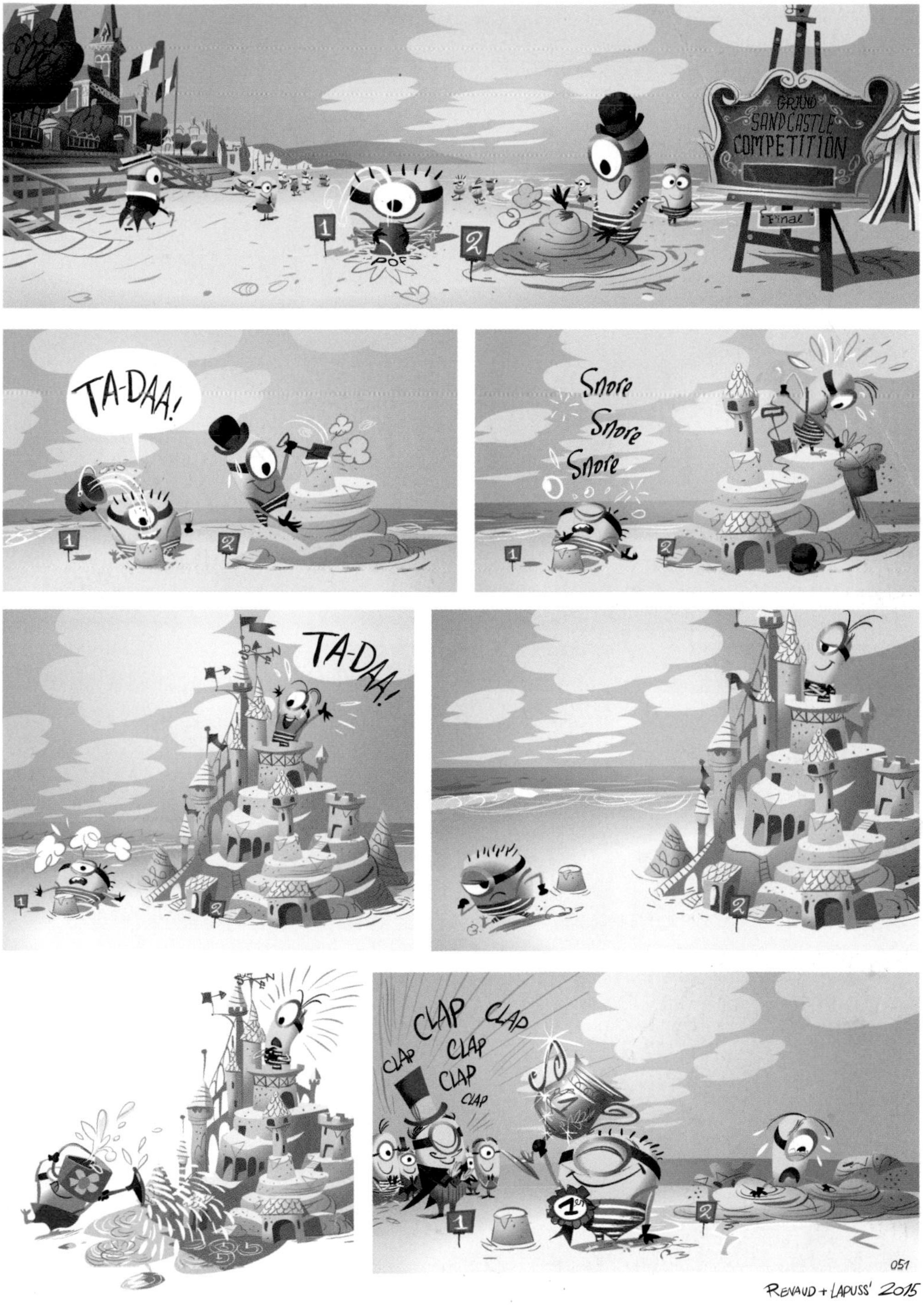
GRAND SANDCASTLE COMPETITION
Final
POF
TA-DAA!
Snore
Snore
Snore
TA-DAA!
CLAP
CLAP
CLAP
CLAP
CLAP
CLAP
1st

RENAUD + LAPUSS' 2015

BEAUTIFUL COCONUT

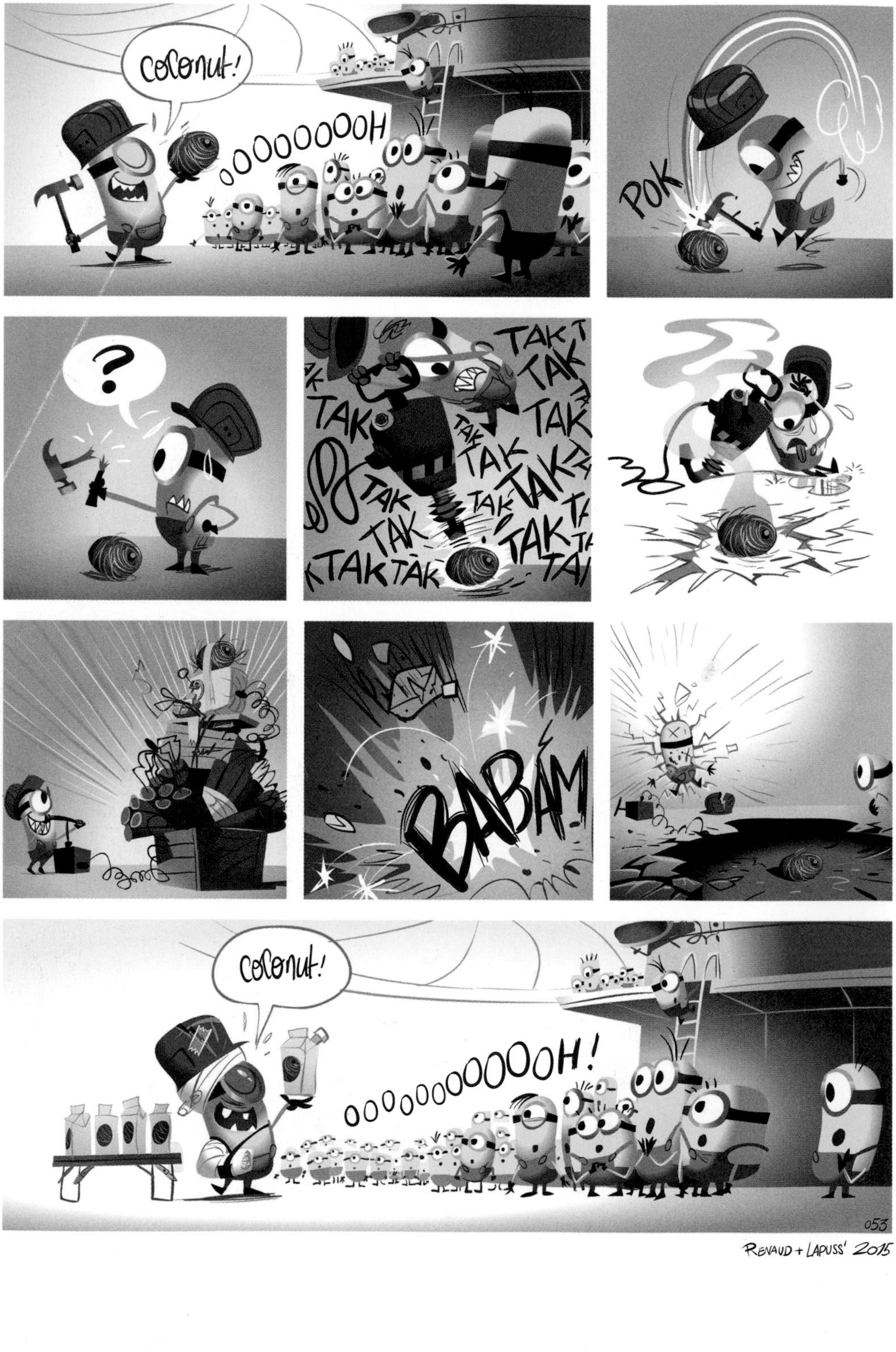
COCONUT!
OOOOOOOOOH
POK
?
TAK TAK TAK TAK TAK TAK TAK TAK TAK TAK TAK TAK TAK
BABAM
COCONUT!
OOOOOOOOOOOOOH!

RENAUD + LAPUSS' 2015

ROCKABILLY BANANA

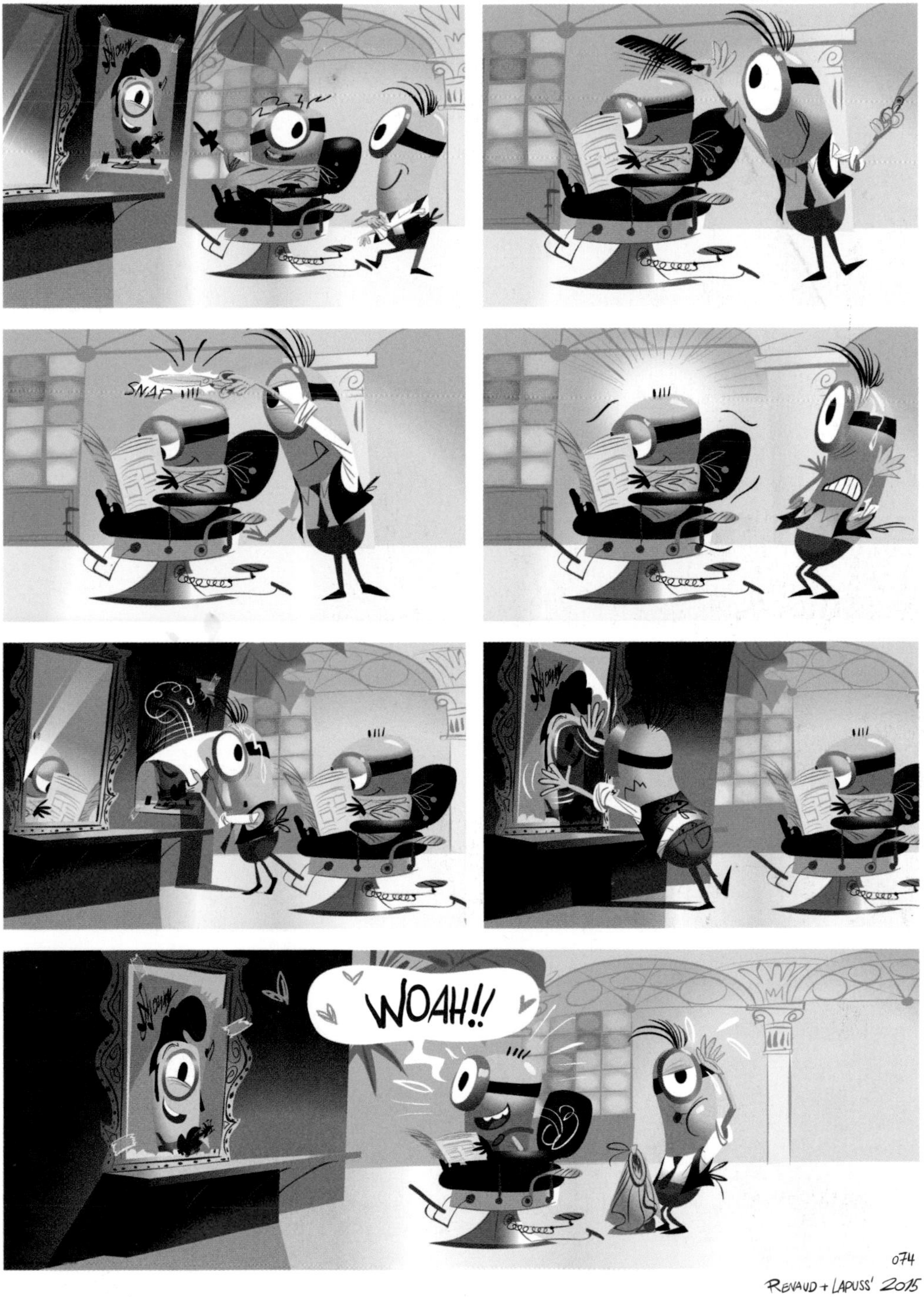

SNAP
WOAH!!

RENAUD + LAPUSS' 2015

FATAL ROT

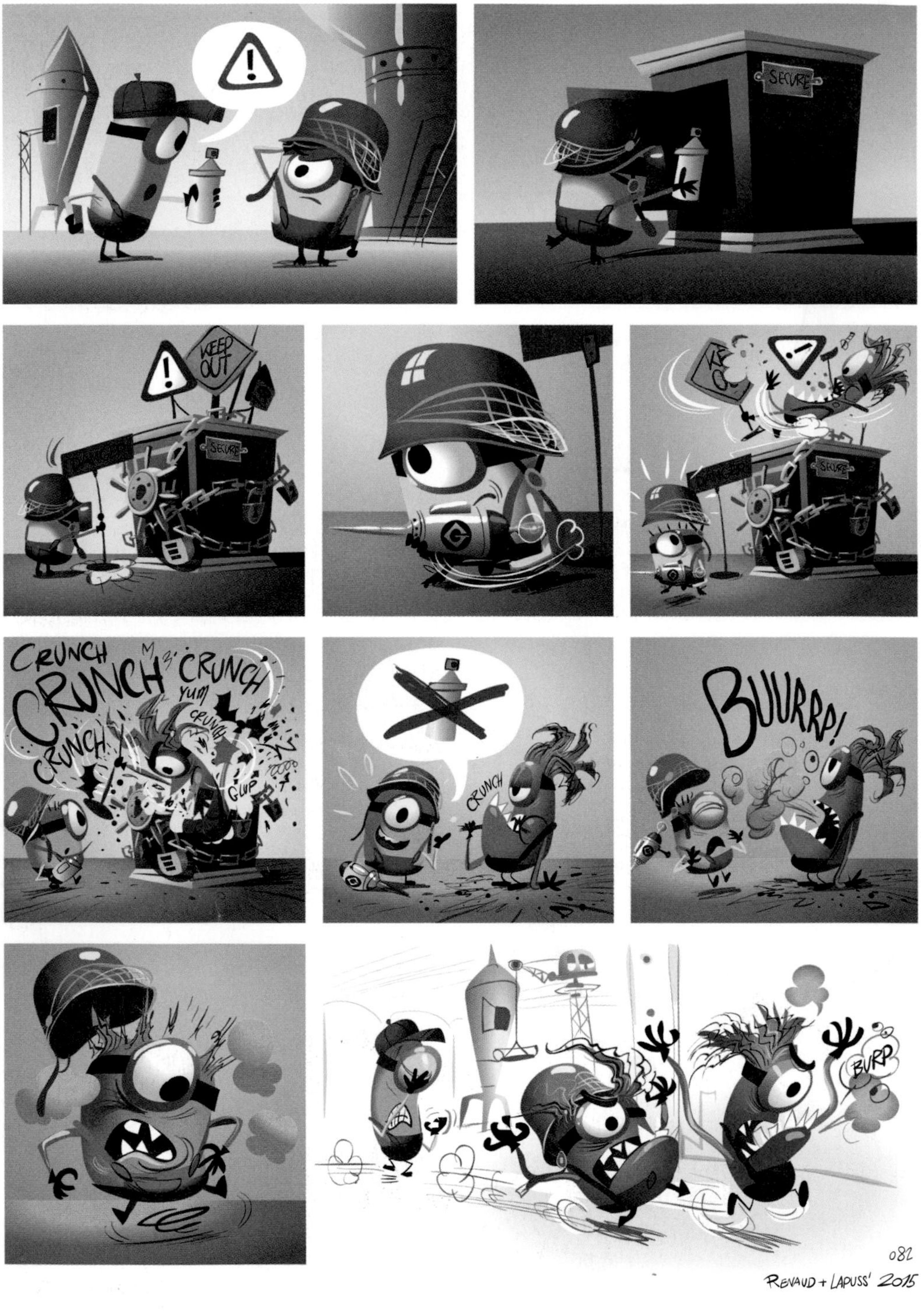
SECURE
KEEP OUT
SECURE
SECURE
CRUNCH
CRUNCH
CRUNCH
CRUNCH
yum
CRUNCH
GLUP
CRUNCH
BUURRP!
BURP

RENAUD + LAPUSS' 2015

ANTIDOTE

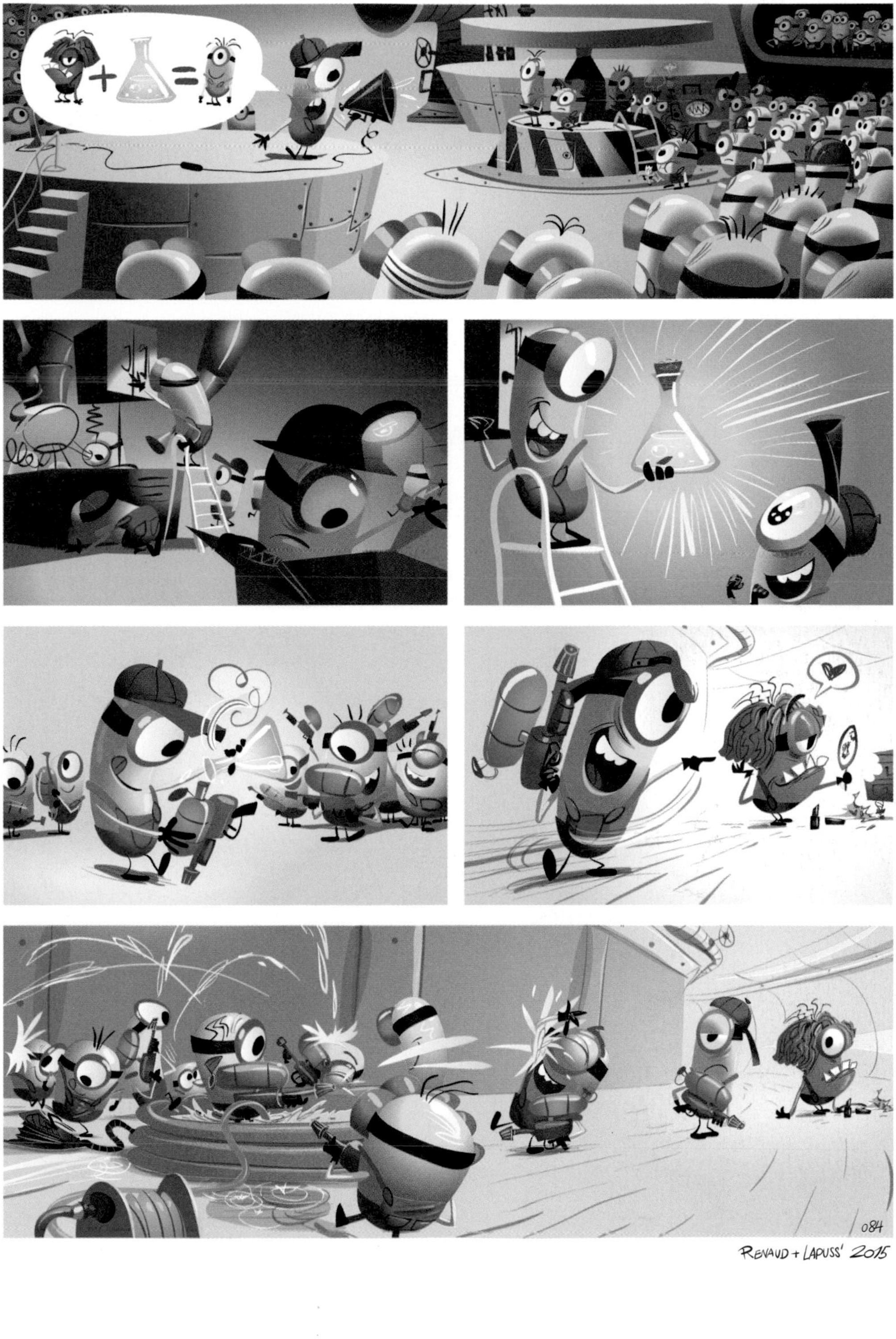

RENAUD + LAPUSS' 2015

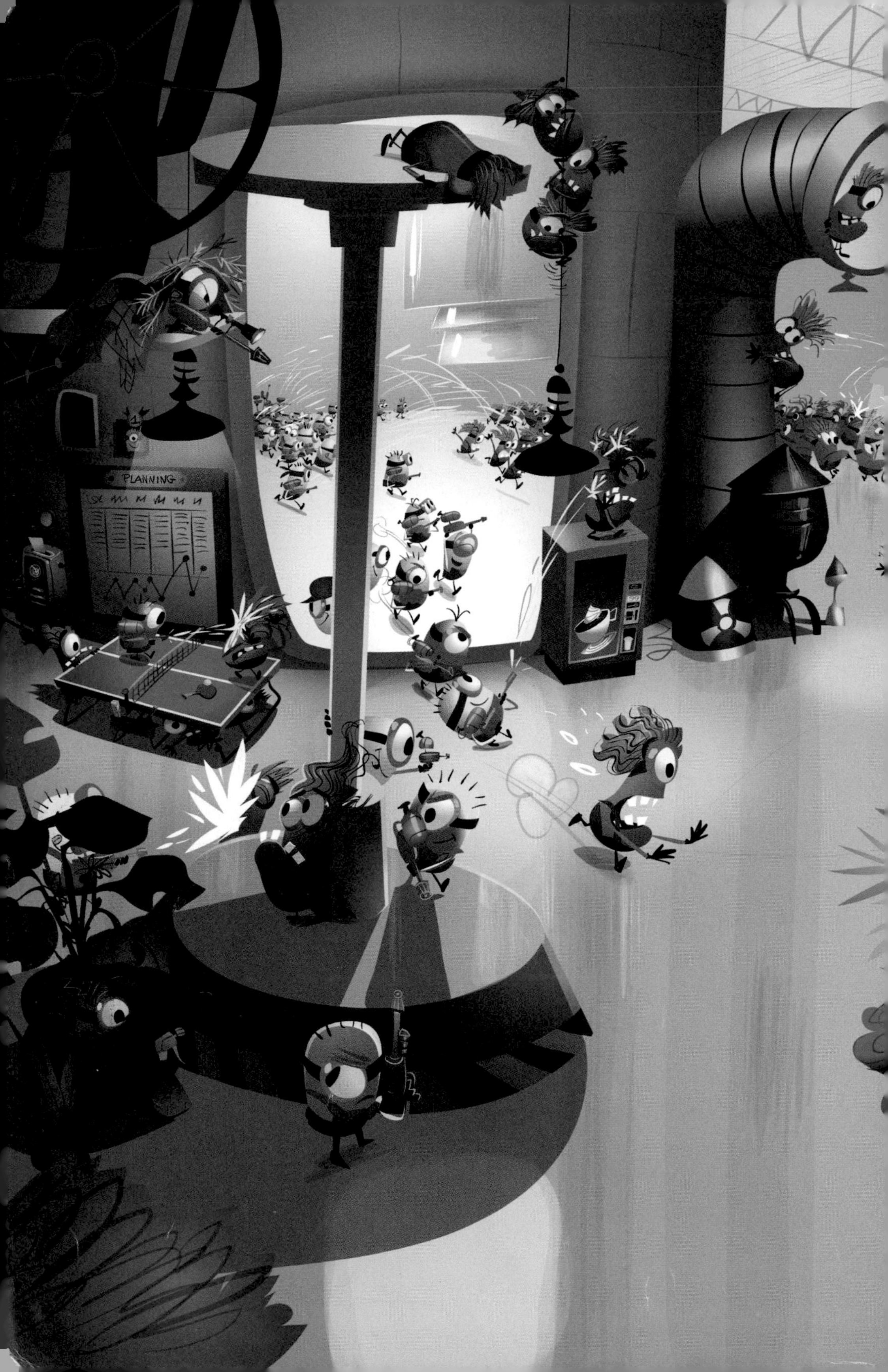
PLANNING

PAINT JOKE

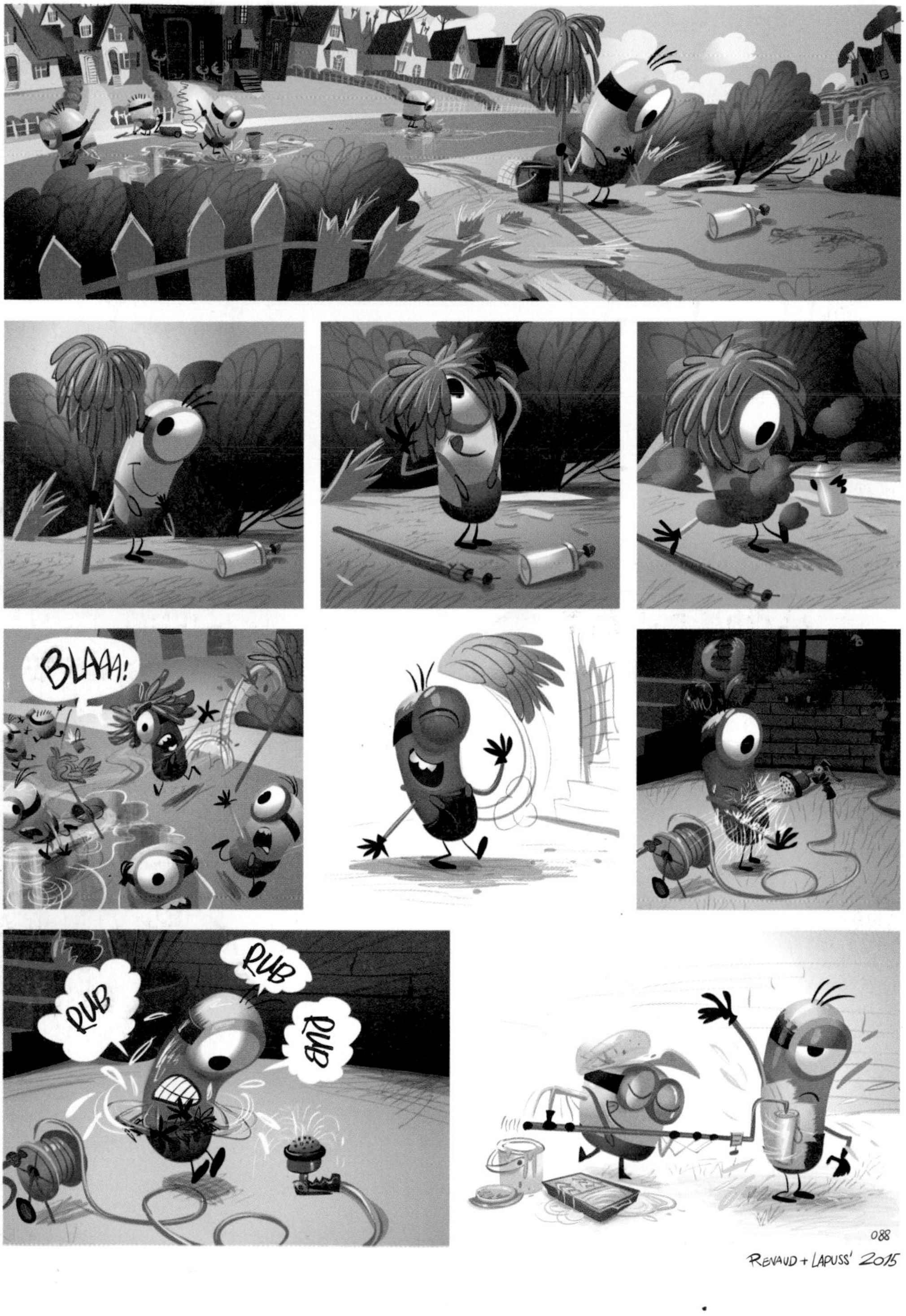
BLAAA!
RUB
RUB
RUB

RENAUD + LAPUSS' 2015

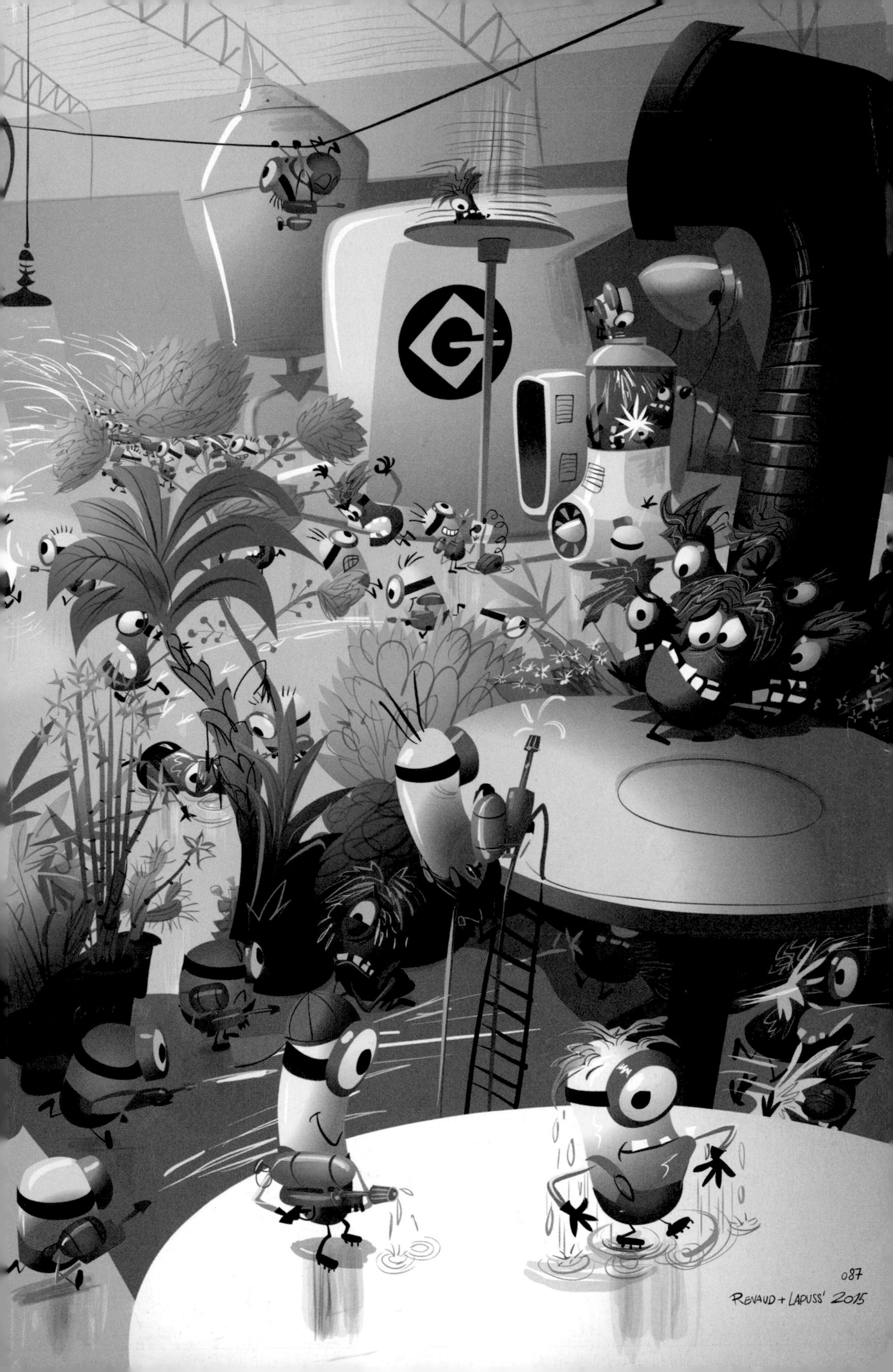
RENAUD + LAPUSS' 2015